Totally Bound Publishing books by Amelia Kingston

So Far, So Good
So, That Got Weird
This is So Happening
So Wrong, it's Wright
So Not My Type

I0544683

So Far, So Good

SO NOT MY TYPE

AMELIA KINGSTON

So Not My Type
ISBN # 978-1-83943-982-7
©Copyright Amelia Kingston 2021
Cover Art by Erin Dameron-Hill ©Copyright May 2021
Interior text design by Claire Siemaszkiewicz
Totally Bound Publishing

SO NOT MY TYPE

Dedication

For my mother
and in loving memory of my grandmothers.
Thank you for teaching me strength, courage and
love in their many different forms.

Chapter One

Jackie

"You can get out of my way or you can die. The choice is yours. You've got to the count of ten," I crow into the mic of my headset. *I love this game.* Destroying egotistical douche canoes in Rule Them All is one of my all-time favorite things. And I'm good at it. I was born to dominate this computer world with an iron fist.

"That time of the month, Trix?" the snotty, barely post-pubescent voice of S3Xk!ng69 rings in my ear. He must be new.

Wrong choice, dipshit. A wicked smile twists my red-stained lips.

"One. Two. Ten. Time's up." With a few keystrokes my digital army squashes my enemies with brutal efficiency.

"Holy shit." The woeful cry is music to my ears. "I was just playing around."

"Awww. Poor baby. Next time you feel like *playing* I suggest you stay the fuck away from Woman'sWorld."

Yes, I named my make-believe country Woman'sWorld. And yes, I have zero remorse in exterminating pests like this one. He can't say I didn't warn him. Rule Them All is not for the timid or insecure. It's a dog-eat-dog world with player-controlled countries clawing at each other to get to the top. To be the best. My gamer handle is DominaTrix for a reason.

"Wow Jackie, that was harsh," my best friend chastises me in our private video chat. Elizabeth is a bleeding heart. I love her to death, but she wants to think the best of everyone. Truth is, some people are just assholes. A little bit of humbling goes a long way.

"He had it coming," her boyfriend, Austin, chimes in. I'd nearly cut his balls off last year when he broke Elizabeth's heart. Believe me, *he* had it coming too. I think he's still trying to get on my good side. I promise I have one. It's just reserved for a very select group of truly amazing people. The rest of the world can fuck right off.

"Thanks, Man Meat. But I don't need your approval." I flip off the camera with a simper. He chuckles, and Elizabeth groans.

"Don't you have to work in like three hours?" she asks.

I glance across my small studio apartment to the clock on the milkcrate that serves as my nightstand. The bright, abrasive, orange 3:00 silently scolds me.

"Shit. Guess tomorrow's going to be a bitch." I shrug, hugging one knee up to my chest, resting my chin on it, and grinning at my best friend through the camera.

She rolls her eyes at me. "Did you at least finish your submission for the contest?"

My gaze darts up to the dozens of half-finished designs taped up on nearly every square inch of wall space.

"Almost," I lie.

"Almost?" She calls me out with the same disappointed tone my mom uses. The sound is like a tiny needle poking me in the eye.

"Yeah, almost. As in just about. Nearly."

"As in no."

"I'll finish it tomorrow." It's a bold-faced lie, and we both know it.

Every year E.B. Jericho, one of my all-time favorite sci-fi writers, holds a contest to design the cover art for her latest release. And every year I promise myself I'll enter. I have a million and one ideas, but I always let the deadline for submission pass me by. I've been torturing myself for months trying to come up with a unique design, but nothing seems right. The fact that this is *the last* book in the series makes it that much more important.

"You better. You've got this thing on lockdown." Elizabeth's faith in me is unwavering, despite the fact that I've never actually had any paid graphic artist work.

I glance over to my long-forgotten drafting table, now housing junk mail and yet-to-be-folded laundry. I haven't used it or any of my hundreds of dollars' worth of design software since I gave up on starting my own graphic design business a couple years ago. In the six short months after I dropped out of college, I realized selling my art meant selling a piece of my soul with it. I was a used car salesman every time I tried for a commission. *I'm really talented, I swear. Trust me.*

Rejection after rejection poured in until I just stopped trying. After a long morning of slinging coffee, doodling cover design ideas is all I have the energy for.

"You've read every one of his books, what? Like a dozen times?" Elizabeth asks.

"*Her* books and at least a dozen," I correct her.

No one really knows who E.B. Jericho is. She's a notorious recluse, but Elizabeth and I have a standing bet on the author's gender. She goes with odds, seeing as how seventy-five percent of sci-fi writers are men. I am convinced E.B. is a woman. She's too clever and witty not to be. If we ever met, we'd be hetero-lifemates. Instant besties for sure.

"All right, kiddos. I better get my beauty sleep." I blow a kiss at the screen.

"Night, Jackie," Austin's deep voice announces.

"Night. Love you, babe," Elizabeth chirps with a sweet smile.

"Love you too."

I click off the camera, toss my glasses onto my desk and shut down my computer. Stretching my arms up and taking a long, deep breath, I sweep my eyes over the design ideas splattering my walls again. *Not one of them is good enough.* It's so late it's early, but my mind is still racing. The idea of submitting a design to be judged by someone I truly admire makes me nauseous.

I grab my sketchbook and sprawl out in my tangled mess of an unmade bed. Closing my eyes, I picture Persei Rivera, the main character from E.B. Jericho's *Sins of Tomorrow* series. She's a space smuggler and the most kickass character of all time. She's standing tall in front of her ship, *Phobos*, a Hellhound-class light space cruiser. Her grease-stained cargo pants are tucked into lunar-dust speckled boots. Her father's old leather bomber jacket is zipped up to keep out the chill on the darkside of the deserted space rock where she's currently stowing cargo. The wind blows her raven-black hair in thick waves behind her, and her pale skin appears nearly translucent. The low light from a distant sun glints off the laser pistol strapped to her hip. Her arms are crossed, and the edge of her mouth is quirked up in a devious challenge. She's the Dirty Harry of space. She *wants* you to try something. *Punk.*

In my mind, the sight is clear as day. I spring my eyes open and stare down at the blank page. Two strokes of my pen and it's already gone wrong. I rip the page out of my sketchbook, crumple it into a tiny ball and toss it across the room with a huff. I try again, but I can't get the angle right for *Phobos*. She's an impressive ship, and *I* made her look like a bathtub toy! Another page ripped out. Another discarded failure.

Over and over again, I doodle the same intergalactic scene until my eyelids get heavy and I pass out in a heap of crumpled paper.

* * * *

The obnoxious beeping of my alarm startles me awake. With a loud groan and a quick kick, I send the institutionalized torture device flying across the room. The beeping gets softer, sadder, before finally stopping. I'm the wrong way round in my bed on top of the covers. I pick my head up and the crinkling of paper echoes in my ear. I stare down at my latest creation, the sleek starship smudged and ruined with my drool. *Great.* I swipe the whole mess into a pile on the floor. I'm back asleep before I can regret the half-conscious decision.

Untold hours later, I'm stirred awake again by the less-than-gentle but very familiar poke of a wooden cane in my side. I push it away and roll over, but the poking persists.

"What?" I whine.

"Oh, so you are alive." The bed dips beside me, and I crack my eyes open to stare up at Pops' sly smile. "I was beginning to think it was just the wistful delusion of an old man that I had a brilliant and punctual granddaughter."

I flop onto my back and stretch out my arms and legs, curling my toes with a satisfied moan.

"Brilliant, sure. Punctual, not so much."

Pops hums. "A man can dream. But now it's time for you to face the day. Life goes on whether you're living it or not, my love," he quips, with a final poke in the ribs for good measure.

"Yes, sir." I give him a two-finger salute and a huge smile. With an achy groan, he stands and strides to the door. "Did you take your pills?" I call to his retreating back.

"Get to work, young lady," he snips playfully.

"Take your pills, old man," I yell back.

Pops and I each have an apartment above his coffee shop, so luckily my commute is easy. Fifteen minutes later I'm downstairs, unlocking the door and waiting for the morning to be over.

I pick up the copy of *Honourbound* I have stashed in a special secret cubby hole under the register. I thumb gently through the well-worn pages, picturing my favorite scenes as the pages fly by in a blur. It is the fifth and most recent book in the *Sins of Tomorrow* series. It came out six months ago, and I've already lost count of how many times I've read it. I don't bother with a bookmark, letting fate decide what adventure Persei will take me on today. I stop at a random page, lean against the counter and get to reading.

It's barely after eight o'clock when my phone buzzes with an incoming call in the front pocket of my apron. There's only one person who actually calls me, and I'm not in the headspace to deal with her and her passive-aggressive guilt-trip right now. Without looking, I send my mom to voicemail, knowing there's not a chance in hell I'll actually listen to her message. Two minutes later my phone buzzes with an incoming text. I make the mistake of reading it, despite knowing it'll be more nagging.

Robert is looking for someone to design a logo for his new brokerage. Just something simple, so I'm sure you could manage it. Call him. This is a great opportunity.

Below the text is a picture of a guy's business card. It's basic and boring. Boxy black lettering and bold font makes it look like a standard template. There's zero personality. Zero wow factor. Real Estate brokers aren't the most exciting bunch, but I almost feel sorry for this guy. I slip *Honourbound* back into its special place, making sure to cover it with a plastic menu in case of accidental coffee spillage.

I grab a napkin and sketch out a few possible logos for Robert the Real Estate Broker. They are simple and elegant—given he's a friend of my mom's I doubt he'll want anything flashy. I'm lost in my work with a small smile on my face when a snide voice interrupts me.

"Excuse me," the voice says in that condescending tone rich people reserve for lowly service industry types.

I look up from my sketch to find a woman about my age, late twenties, glaring at me with contempt and clearly annoyed I've wasted a precious minute of her time.

"If you're done *doodling*, I'm ready to order."

I crumple up the doodled-on napkin in my fist and throw it on the ground. *It was trash anyway.*

"What do you want?" My tone is flat. She's not our usual customer. We cater more to the eccentric free spirits of the world.

She scoffs, her displeasure at having to be here instead of in a Starbucks evident in her sour pout and not-so-subtle head shake. "Venti cappuccino."

"*Large* cappuccino is five-seventy-five," I rattle off, clicking a few buttons on our ancient register.

She hands me a twenty. I hand her back her change, which she takes the time to count with a watchful eye before she sashays away. I suppress a gag. I take my aggression out on the coffee grounds, putting my body weight into tamping them down with a wide smile. The espresso shot comes out thick as mud and smelling like a burnt tire.

"Cappuccino," I yell.

She takes a sip and I laugh at the sight of her nearly doing a spit-take. She shakes her head, looking me up and down, her judgmental gaze lingering on my nose ring and tattoos. My bright red hair is thrown up in a messy bun because I was too lazy to deal with bed head. My black T-shirt is wrinkled but clean. *I think.* There are coffee stains on my jeans and ink stains on my fingers. Compared to her fresh blowout, sharp pants suit and French manicure, I'm a hot mess. The look of disgust on her face makes me wish I'd added a little *special sauce*. I mean spit.

"You really should get your act together if you want to be taken seriously."

I bite my tongue, shoving down the urge to tell her to go fuck herself. This is Pops' place after all.

With a hair toss, she's nearly out the door when I shout, "Want my mom's number? You'd get along great!"

I mutter angrily to myself for letting some stranger get under my skin. I'm a damn good graphic designer. An artist. She can shove that cappuccino up her bleached asshole for all I care.

My new indignant rage fuels my motivation. I pull out my phone and scroll through E.B. Jericho's Instagram page. She has a new post every day with a countdown for the contest. There are exactly forty-seven days left until my cover design has to be submitted for a chance to win. I suppress the familiar panic churning in my stomach.

Fuck it.

This is my year. I'm going to win this thing if it kills me.

Chapter Two

Eddie

I hike my laptop bag up on my shoulder and stare at the hand-painted *"Beans & Dreams"* sign.

"Why am I here again?" I ask my best friend on the other side of our video call and frown at the cutesy logo. Not the place I'd usually grab my cup of morning courage, but Benji's been a royal pain about it. He's nagged me every day for the past week, insisting I check the place out but not really saying why he thinks it's so special.

"Because you needed to get out of that apartment."

"That is a faulty premise, my friend."

Benji shakes his head and lets out an exasperated chuckle. He's been harping on me for a full two weeks to get out and about. I finally gave in and I'm already regretting it.

"You do know a whole entire world exists *outside* your apartment, right? The *real* world?"

"Do you know *real* is often overrated?"

It's a recurring theme of our friendship. Benji pushes me to live in the "real world" and I fight him tooth and nail. He's worried about me becoming a total shut-in, but I don't know why. I'm a happy little recluse. Everything I need I can have delivered to my front door. My imagination provides more than enough of a distraction to life's monotony.

Still, to make my best friend happy, I trekked out to this funky little coffee shop. Benji is on the other end of the phone to make sure I'm actually here. I've been known to make up a story or two.

"You'll like this place, I promise." Benji smiles like the cat that ate the canary.

I crook an eyebrow and glare at him on my phone's screen. *Fat chance.* I'm here to appease him, so he'll leave it alone for a while, but I'm under no illusion of actually enjoying this little excursion.

"Dude, have I ever led you astray?" Benji asks. At my incredulous look, he quickly adds, "Other than that thing with paintball. And the slam poetry. And the timeshare scam."

"And the nudist colony." He winces at the mention of the worst of all his ill-advised suggestions.

"Okay, that one wasn't my fault. I thought 'naturalist' meant Bear Grylls not bare ass."

"If only there was some way to research these ideas. Some sort of world-wide web of information..."

"Fine. I'll admit it. I've messed up a few times."

"Seven," I fake cough into my hand. *Why do I still give in to his stupid outing ideas?* Probably because he's still trying when most everyone else in my life has given up. *And I'm a glutton for punishment.*

"But this is lucky number eight. I promise you're going to like it."

I groan in disbelief and pull the door open. The smell of dark roast envelops me as I step into the funky little shop. I pause to take a deep lungful. I love that smell. My blood pumps faster through my veins, as if the caffeine seeps into my system through the scent alone. I step farther inside with a satisfied hum. So far, this is the best of Benji's idiotic adventures, although that's admittedly a pretty low bar. Every month or so he cajoles me into soloing some new experience. He claims doing it alone forces me to be engaged, but really I think he finds the stories of my awkward discomfort hilarious.

A little hole in the wall shimmied between two large old buildings, this place is determined to exist despite its blatant inappropriateness. It's a small space with only four colorful but mismatched tables filling the long and narrow interior. I wouldn't be surprised to find the Mad Hatter holding a tea party in the corner. The counter and display case take up a full quarter of it. *Cozy*.

One wall is smothered with assorted eclectic knick-knacks and hodge-podge photos. It looks like someone's scrapbook threw up all over it, only less organized. There's a faded *Cats* playbill next to a random laminated receipt for a cucumber sandwich and an antique cuckoo clock. Whoever decorated this place needs to go back to design school. The clutter makes me cringe. I want to strip it down and paint the whole thing a nice, soothing soft gray. I look away before my OCD kicks in.

Mercifully, the longer, far wall isn't the same disaster. It's covered in a detailed mural that knocks me for a loop. I recognize it instantly. It's the final scene from *Honourbound* where Persei stands shattered but victorious over Fornax. It's like someone ripped the image straight out of my head. It's absolutely *awesome*.

"Wow." I audibly gasp. "You seeing this?" I flip to the rear camera on my phone and show Benji the full mural.

"Told you. That's not in your apartment."

"I kind of wish it was." I've got a bewildered smile on my face, taking in every detail of the mural. I've got to hand it to Benji—for once I'm glad I made the trip.

"Something tells me that's not the only thing you'll end up wanting to take home."

"Huh?"

"Go get a coffee, genius. Remember, you've gotta stay for at least an hour. Your apartment will still be there when you get back."

"Yeah, yeah. Call you later."

After taking a couple of photos, I tear my eyes off the spectacular mural, tuck my phone back in my pocket and stride over to place an order.

The barista is leaning against the counter casually, her eyes fixated on the paperback clutched in her ink-stained fingers. I recognize the latest E.B. Jericho cover immediately. That makes sense, given the mural.

Her distraction affords me the rare pleasure of studying her. I'm a student of human nature. The irony is that while I'm not too keen on interacting with people, I love to watch them. To figure out what makes them tick. *What are her deepest desires? Her darkest fears?*

Her scarlet-red hair turns orange at the tips and makes her look like a living fireball. The glint of a nose ring and a mischievous grin make me wonder if she's got a wicked sense of humor. Thick black Buddy Holly-style glasses draw my attention to her eyes, focused and attentive.

I clear my throat.

She doesn't look up. Instead, she holds out the index finger of her left hand and keeps reading. Her short nails are painted blue with colorful splattering that makes them look galactic. The finger is smudged with a deep black ink, and I'm curious to know it's origin. To know her story.

Benji was right. *For once.*

Unrushed, she flips to the next page. I shove my hands in my pockets and watch her with a goofy smile on my face.

"Good morn—" I lean forward to garner her attention, but don't manage to get the salutation out before those slender fingers pinch my lips closed. The bizarre intimacy of a stranger's hand on my face is heightened by the fact that she still hasn't bothered to look at me. I'm in shock. I stand there, shushed like an infant by this woman I've never met. Waiting to be allowed to speak, I'm too surprised to be angry.

I catch the whiff of something sugary. *Caramel.* She smells sweet when she seems to be anything but. The intimate moment passes. She nestles a bookmark between the pages, tucks the book lovingly under the counter and turns her attention to me.

I take advantage of my first opportunity to read the white lettering written across her black shirt. *Does running out of fucks count as cardio?* I guess I was right about that wicked sense of humor.

"Welcome to Beans & Dreams. What can I get you?" she asks, her tone uninterested but not openly hostile.

"Oh, so this *is* a coffee shop? I thought I stumbled into the library, what with all the reading and the…shushing." The corner of my mouth quirks up, amused by my own joke.

"Yep, it's a coffee shop. But it can easily become a murder scene." Her voice is thick and sweet like caramel and her smile innocent despite the death threat. Customer service is clearly not her strong suit.

"Large coffee. Two sugars." I decide not to poke the red-headed bear.

"Three-fifty." She snatches the five-dollar bill out of my hand and makes change.

Just as she turns away to make my coffee, I add, "Hold the spit."

I expect an eye roll, but instead her ruby lips curl up into the hint of an amused smile. She mimics swishing spit around her mouth, scrunches up her face and swallows hard. After the ridiculous show, she gives me a thumbs-up. What is this bizarre little place? *Is this how Alice felt falling down that rabbit hole?*

I take a seat at one of the empty tables, positioning myself to have a clear view of the mural. It's a simple coincidence I have a great view of her standing at the register as well.

Feeling inspired by the quirky, mystical atmosphere of this place, I start up my laptop, eager to get to work. I stare up at the amazing mural and my mind spins off into a million different ideas. I stare at it for minutes at a time, studying every inch of the scrawling painting. It is oddly mesmerizing. The detail. The precision. The care. Whoever painted it must love Persei Rivera as much as I do.

"Khakis," the barista's voice calls out.

My gaze snaps up, and I look around the coffee shop. I'm the only one here.

"Khakis."

My gaze falls to my lap, and I look at my pressed tan slacks. Paired with a pale-blue button down, it's my standard attire. Business casual is nearly always appropriate and an easy way to go unnoticed. Apparently, in a funky coffee shop, I'm the oddball.

I meet her eyes, my eyebrows pinching together. I point to myself. And mouth, "*Me?*"

Her head tilts to the side and her gaze traces over me, taking in my smart-casual button down and crisp khakis. She nods with a twinkle in her eyes and a *no shit, Sherlock* look on her face. She's fighting to keep a smile at bay. I walk to the counter and take my coffee.

"Thanks."

"You're very welcome, Khakis," she answers with a teasing lilt.

She stands there watching me, apparently entertained by something. I'll be damned if I can figure out what. I take a sip, sucking in a loud breath when the burnt bitterness hits my tongue.

"That's...robust."

"Can't handle it strong?" she challenges.

"Strong I'm fine with. It's the thick and...gritty I'm not used to."

"Gritty?" She narrows her eyes and puckers her mouth like she's trying to make my head explode telepathically. When the corners of her mouth curl up, I know she's settled on her snarky retort. I wait for it like a tennis pro preparing for the next volley.

"I believe you're enjoying our signature espresso garnish, meant for the stoutest of coffee connoisseurs. I suppose your pallet isn't as refined as I anticipated."

"Your *garnish* is grounds for an assault charge on my taste buds. I've never had to chew my coffee before."

Her nostrils flare, and I smile. This woman is a ball buster, and I rather enjoy the instant karma of throwing it right back at her.

"All part of the unique experience we strive to bring our customers here at Beans & Dreams. Plus, I bet you can't even taste the spit."

My second sip of coffee sputters out of my mouth making her laugh. I choke it back, wiping the drops off my chin with my eyes wide and bewildered. I can't for the life of me think of a clever comeback. Instead, I stare at the coffee vixen completely dumbfounded.

Satisfied, she simpers and walks away.

"I like your shirt," I blurt out, not quite ready for our verbal sparring to be over.

She turns back to look at me and tilts her head, like she's trying to figure out if I'm serious or about to land a punchline.

"Thanks?" Her voice goes up, as if she's asking a question.

"You're welcome." I tip my coffee cup to her. "I'm Eddie." I hold out my hand. She doesn't shake it, so I wave. *Why would I wave? Who does that?* "And thanks for my *unique* coffee garnish."

Finally having enough, she shakes her head, turns and waves me away over her shoulder. I watch her walk away and my mind starts racing. Ideas pile up in my head like a freeway during rush hour. Not wanting my sudden inspiration to go to waste, I scurry back to my table and get to work, keeping a watchful eye on my new muse.

Chapter Three

Jackie

I was right. Today has been a bitch. The morning was just slow enough to drive me crazy and too busy for me to actually get any real reading done. A steady trickle of customers has tormented me, including the pair of khakis that's been here almost as long as I have. I swear, he was trying to piss me off earlier, but after he finally sat down and shut up, he's innocuous.

I feel his eyes tracing me most of the day as I fiddle with something behind the counter or shuffle around the shop. Usually, I'd call a guy out for that kind of thing, but weirdly enough it doesn't bother me. His focused gaze is more curious excitement than creepy leering. Like a kid standing in line for the roller coaster, despite knowing full well they're too short to ride. I figured he'd get the hint when I ignored him for hours on end. *Guess not.*

He's been glued to that seat. Concentrated. Fastidious. Dedicated. It's actually kind of impressive.

That's how I get when I'm drawing. Other than watching me, he's been content to keep to himself, laser-focused on his computer. *I wonder if he's actually an android?* I chuckle at the idea of Khakis being released into the world to see if he can pass for human. His own little Turing test.

I glance over at him. He smiles and waves, only his hand moving with a bend at the wrist while the rest of him is stock still. *Waves.* Who does that? *Robots pretending to be human, that's who.*

I grab a napkin and sketch what Khakis looks like under those starched pants, all gears and wires. A meat grinder for a stomach, a filament lightbulb for a brain, and an old-timey pocket watch where his heart should be. I'm lost in my little steampunk doodle and don't notice he's packed up his laptop and come to stand next to me at the counter.

"Been thinking about me without my clothes on?" he asks with a self-conscious smile. It's a pick-up line, and a decent one if I'm honest, but his soft voice and questioning eyes make me think he doesn't have much experience flirting. Poor guy has no idea he's playing with fire.

"Just wondering if you'll pass your Turing test." I shrug and slip the napkin doodle into my book.

"If you're wondering, haven't I already failed? And for the record, my heart should totally be a calculator watch."

I stand up straight, cross my arms, and stare at him. I'm surprised he knows that the Turing test is to see if a robot can pass as human. *Bonus points to Khakis.* I can't make up my mind if that makes him more or less likely to be an android.

The obnoxious cuckoo clock chimes and two rosy-cheeked, lederhosen-clad men pop out, spin around, dip forward, smooch, then disappear back into their holes. *No pun intended.* Pops got it in Germany decades ago. He adores the thing, despite the fact that it drives me bonkers.

After my grandma died, Pops disappeared for a few months. I was too young to remember, but Mom says he was traveling around Europe "discovering himself". Whatever the hell that means. It's great Pops took the time to figure himself out, but Mom's still got her panties in a twist over it. Add it to the very long list of things I can't talk to her about.

I love Pops, but I have to agree with my mom for once. That clock is kitschy, loud and annoying. Usually I hate the thing, but today it's music to my ears. That hideous clang means it's noon. *Thank God!* I'm so ready for this day to be over. I just want to crawl back into bed and sleep for the rest of my life. I stretch my back and groan before grabbing a rag and wiping down the counter.

"Long day?" Khakis asks.

"Same number of hours as every other one, I'm pretty sure." I keep cleaning with my back to him.

"I recall reading somewhere that time is relative." His tone is flat. Neutral, even though he's teasing me. For some reason that is infuriating.

"Aren't you clever."

"I have my moments."

"I'll let you in on a little secret." I twist to face him and mock whisper, "This isn't one of them."

"Oh, I don't know. I happen to think I'm pretty charming." He gives me a boyish grin that is *undeniably* charming. *Damn it.*

"I take it back—you're right. Time *is* relative. And you know what makes it just drag on forever? Guys who just won't take a hint." The room is thick with my sarcasm.

Without missing a beat, he retorts, "Well, you're such a delight. I can hardly blame 'em." Khakis shrugs and gives me a little nod.

Touché.

"Who wouldn't be in a good mood after hours of smiling like an asshat and chatting about asinine nonsense?" My voice is light and playful. I give him a gigantic toothy smile.

He clears his throat to cover up a chuckle.

"I was thinking, you should add 'service with a sneer' to all your signage. That's how the saying goes right?"

"That's it, Khakis." I toss down my rag and stomp around the counter to him, unsure of what I'll do when I get there. I only realize how tall he is when I'm toe-to-toe and have to crane my neck to see him. He's not particularly broad or muscular, but he's a lot more solid now that I'm all up in his business. He smells clean, like he stepped right out of a laundry detergent commercial. It has me a little disoriented. Instead of tearing him a new one, I stand there like a dumbass, staring into his dark eyes and struggling to remember what I was so pissed about.

"Hola, chica!" JC's cheery voice rings through the small shop as his over-the-top personality fills every inch of the space. The other barista Pops hired is my opposite in every possible way—male, gay, Puerto Rican, piercing-free and too nice for his own good. On days like today, he is my very own personal ray of sunshine.

JC comes to a screeching halt at the sight of Khakis and me facing off. I don't know why he is surprised.

He's seen me lose it on customers before. Today is nothing special.

"Oh, sorry." JC blushes softly. "Am I interrupting something?"

"Only a pending homicide," I quip and release Khakis from my death stare. He chuckles, a low and surprisingly masculine sound rattling out of his chest. I was not expecting that. Or the way the sound made my skin tingle like an idiot teenager with a stupid crush.

I skip over to JC and wrap him in a giant bear hug.

"I've never been so happy to see you!" I pull back and plant a quick kiss on his lips. He's slightly taller than me with curly black hair, chocolate eyes and smooth tan skin. He's like a pocket Ricky Martin.

Khakis skirts around us and slips out the door without a word. *Victory is mine.*

I release JC and walk back over to the counter.

"Who was that?" he asks, his voice high-pitched and betraying his excitement.

"Nobody." I shrug and snag my book and purse from under the counter.

"Nobody? That's why you couldn't resist mauling my face in front of him?"

I scoff. "First of all, I didn't maul anything. That was a very respectful kiss. And second, it's been a crap day and I'm happy you're here. It means I can take off."

"You're a bad liar, Red." He crosses his arms and shakes his head at me. "You looked ready to climb his ass like a Sherpa on Everest."

"He's just a customer. Don't be dramatic."

"Girl, please. Dramatic is my middle name."

"Your middle name is Fernando."

"I'm having it legally changed. And you can't tell me there weren't sparks flying between you and Mr. Clean Cut."

"Don't be an ass. That was annoyance, not attraction. I'm sure I'll never see Khakis again."

JC groans and stalks off, tired of debating when he knows I'll never admit to enjoying arguing with a pair of khakis. *Just the teeny tiniest bit.* I will say one thing for Khakis, he made an otherwise crap day somewhat interesting. But it's not like he makes my lady bits tingle, or my nipples get hard. It's not like I've got a bucket of adrenaline coursing through my body and no mountain to climb.

Chapter Four

Eddie

It's two in the morning, and I've given up counting sheep and am now inventorying the whole damn farm. My bed is comfortable and my apartment quiet, but my mind won't settle. Anxious energy is coursing through my body, keeping me wide awake. I'm always like this when I'm starting a new project, the ideas swirling around in a jumble, demanding I take the time to sort them out.

By the time four o'clock rolls around, I give up on farm animals and get out of bed. But I'm too restless to be productive. Three separate times I've sat down at my desk and tried to force myself to get some serious work done. No luck. I've paced the length of my penthouse a dozen times and still can't get my mind to focus. I'm cagey and there's only one thing I can think of to fix it.

For the second day in a row, I pack up my laptop and set out. This time, I know a bit more about what

I'm getting myself into when I make my way back to Beans & Dreams. I hustle along the crowded sidewalk, eager to see what the world's worst barista has in store for me today.

"Khakis!" a man's high-pitched voice rings out the minute I step into the quirky coffee shop. I stifle a groan at the obnoxious nickname. And the fact that it's not coming from an angry redhead.

The shop patrons, consisting of a college-aged couple in the corner and an older man sitting by himself, turn to look at me. I give an awkward wave and debate taking a bow. The guy comes rushing up to me. He's in slim-fit capri jeans and a short-sleeve button-down covered in little pink flamingos wearing sunglasses. I recognize him. He's the one who locked lips with the female barista I spent the day watching. I cringe, waiting to be admonished for fighting with his girl. Or were we flirting? *Is flirt-fighting a thing? Flighting?*

Instead of being mad, he seems happy to see me. Giddy even.

"I'm Jesús." He holds out his hand, and I shake it. But before I'm able to introduce myself, he squeezes hard and tugs me along to where the older man is sitting. "And you are coming with me. Pops! Pops, this is the guy I was telling you about."

Jesús gives me a shove in the back and presents me to Pops like I'm here for inspection. Pops sets aside his newspaper and studies me. I very much regret leaving my apartment at this point. Both times I've come into this shop, I've been greeted by the weirdest people in the strangest ways.

"The one from the dating app? With the…piercing?" Pops asks, motioning to his lap.

My jaw drops when I realize the old man with bifocals is asking if I have a pierced cock. *Seriously, how is this place even still in business?*

"Oh God, no!" Jesús giggles behind me, amused I was mistaken for his latest hook-up. *Guess she isn't his girl.* "This is the one your granddaughter looked like she was going to stuff and mount yesterday when I came in to work."

"Excuse me?" I turn to Jesús, who's biting his lip and wiggling his eyebrows, as if there were any doubt what he was trying to insinuate. I shake my head and turn back to Pops. "That's not exactly accurate."

Pops hums and nods. "Which part, the stuffing or the mounting?"

"Either. Neither," I stutter. "Well, maybe the stuffing, but there was definitely no mounting."

"Shame."

"Sorry?" I'm so confused. Does this guy actually want me to have sex with his granddaughter?

"It'd do her good to fall in love. And you're the sort she'd never see coming." Pops stands up and tucks his folded newspaper under his arm. I step back so he can slide around the table. Squaring up in front of me, he places a hand on my shoulder and looks deep into my eyes. "Remember, son, pitch no woo, get no whoopie. I'm heading upstairs, Jesús."

"Okay, Pops," Jesús calls from back behind the counter. "Catch you later."

I'm standing there, in the middle of this coffee shop, reeling from the second bizarre interaction in as many visits. I stumble over to the same table I had yesterday and plop down in the bench seat. I replay the whole interaction with Pops in my head, trying to figure out if that really happened.

"What can I get for you, sweetheart?" Jesús asks, drawing me out of my stupor.

"Who was that? *What* was that?" I ask.

Jesús displays his perfect teeth in a wide smile. "That's Pops. This is his place. Isn't he the best?"

"Interesting, for sure. And the woman from yesterday is his granddaughter?"

"Yep. Apple didn't fall far, am I right?" He gives me a friendly pat on my shoulder.

I pull my laptop out of my bag and start to get situated. Now that I've gone through all that, I better get some quality work out of it.

"Pops seems a bit less homicidal."

Jesús giggles again. "Ain't that the truth? But Red grows on you."

"So does flesh-eating bacteria," I deadpan.

"Daaaymn!" Jesús snaps his fingers three times in a zigzag. "I think that girl might've found her match." He looks back toward where Pops disappeared and lowers his voice. "You know, she's not as scary as she pretends to be. Red's fierce, but she has the biggest heart. Don't let her chase you away too quick, okay?" He gives my shoulder a squeeze, an encouraging smile on his lips.

"Umm. Okay." Everyone who works here is at least half-crazy. "Can I get a black coffee with two sugars?"

"Coming right up!"

Noticeably less gritty coffee in hand and headphones on, I settle into my work. That lasts all of twenty minutes before someone pulling the chair out across from me draws my attention back to the real world.

"You developing a taste for gritty coffee, Khakis?" Red coos with a lopsided grin. She runs her fingers through her fiery hair, pulling it to one side. It exposes the curve of her neck and draws my eyes along her collarbone down to her chest.

Luckily, I catch my wandering gaze before she does and keep my eyes safely above her shoulders.

"Not likely. I'm here for the irresistible asylum-esque ambiance."

"Oh, fuck off." She leans back and flips me off with both hands for good measure.

"See? Don't get that at Starbucks." She shakes her head and bites her lip to stifle a laugh. I shift on the bench, finding myself leaning in closer to her. "I met your Pops."

"I heard." She leans forward across the table, her chin nearly resting on the screen of my laptop. "Sounds like there was some confusion..." Her voice goes soft and sensuous. "So, do you or don't you have a cock piercing?"

"Jesus Christ!" I pinch the bridge of my nose and squeeze my eyes shut.

"You showed it to JC?" She gasps and yells across the cafe, "Hey, JC, is it Prince Albert or a Jacob's Ladder?"

"No, that's not—" I try to off-ramp this colossal miscommunication.

"Prince Albert," Jesús shouts back with a wink.

Red lifts out of her chair to peek at my lap, as if she's going to be able to see the non-existent piercing through my pants.

"Shame. I always wondered what a Jacob's Ladder would feel like," she replies loud enough that Jesús can hear her behind the counter, but her eyes are locked on mine. They are a mesmerizing soft hazel with a mischievous glint. My heart pounds in my chest and my mouth goes dry.

"It's all about how they use it," Jesús answers, shouting over the hiss of steaming milk.

"Ain't that the truth." Red wiggles her eyebrows at me.

"I don't have a dick piercing!" I shout over the both of them, louder than I need to be. The couple in the corner finish their drinks quickly and get out of there, glaring at me like I'm some kind of pervert.

Red saunters over to Jesús and gives him a high-five across the counter. She's wearing the smuggest expression. I stand and stalk over to her, stepping in toe-to-toe. I'm annoyed and frustrated. This woman is infuriating. I open my mouth to give her a piece of my mind, but the power of speech fails me. *This is a first.* I'm never at a loss for words.

"What's wrong, Khakis? Cat got your tongue?" she taunts.

"Listen—" I have no idea what is about to come out of my mouth, but luckily I'm saved by an act of God. Or Jesús, to be more accurate.

"*Dios mio.*" His gasp catches me off guard. His eyes are tearing up and he's focused on the front door.

Red cuts her eyes to the tall, built man in a bespoke suit who just walked in. "What the fuck is *he* doing here?" she growls, anger radiating off her like she's about to ignite.

"I can't..." Jesús's voice is thick with sadness and desperation. "Red, I can't talk to him."

She spins, squeezes Jesús's hand and reaches for something under the counter. An aluminum baseball bat. *Why am I not surprised?*

"Don't worry, JC. I've got this." She slings the bat over her shoulder and walks backward with a wicked smile, looking sexy as hell and more than a bit crazy.

"Are you okay?" I ask Jesús, keeping my voice low and soothing.

"He's my asshole ex," Jesús explains. "That man broke my heart into a million pieces."

Jesús and I watch Red confront the guy. He has to outweigh her by a hundred pounds, but he holds his hands up and looks terrified. I don't blame him. She grabs the lapel of his jacket and pulls him down. She whispers something in his ear, and he turns as white as a sheet. With one quick, withering glance at Jesús, the guy flees out of the front door.

Red turns to face us with a wide smile and blows Jesús a kiss.

"Told you." His voice is soft admiration. "Heart of gold."

"What did you say to him?" I ask, intrigued by the smug look on her face.

"I gave him a vivid description of what it would feel like to have his balls meet my coffee grinder."

I stare at Jesús and shake my head. "Oh yeah, she's a real saint."

Chapter Five

Jackie

"Stalker much?" I call out to Khakis the second he steps into Beans & Dreams for the third day in a row.

He clasps his hand over his heart in mock indignation. "I wouldn't dare."

"Don't tell me you're scared of little ol' me?" I drop my chin to my chest and bat my eyelashes at him. I'm as innocent as fuck.

"If it's all the same to you, I'd prefer my testicles *not* ground into an espresso garnish."

"Then you better behave yourself today." I point a finger at him.

"You aren't too keen on repeat customers, are you? Interesting business model," he quips, undeterred. He takes the same seat as the past two mornings and pulls out his laptop. He is a creature of habit for sure.

"Black, two sugars?" I ask, remembering his order. I'm not as horrible at my job when I actually give a shit.

He nods and adds, "Hold the spit."

"You're no fun, Khakis."

"So I've been told."

The morning flies by in a steady blur of forgettable interactions with faceless customers. Every so often, I check in with Khakis, refilling his coffee without asking and adding it to his running tab for the day. *If he's going to take up a seat all day, he's going to pay for it.*

I watch him when he's deep into whatever he's working on, making these little faces. Pinching his eyes closed tight like he's trying hard to remember something. Shaking his head with a deep sigh as if disappointed with himself. Nodding with a soft hum. *And he thinks I'm crazy?*

I take away his untouched third cup of coffee and set down a fresh fourth when he finally takes a break. He stands and stretches his back, shaking out his arms and legs to get his blood flowing again. I slip back behind the register and pretend I'm reading. He saunters up to the counter and leans down on it, his chin propped in one hand, mirroring my pose. I smash my lips together to fight back a smile.

I can feel his eyes on me, studying my face in the obsessive way he does. I ignore him, enjoying making him wait. I turn a page for show, skimming it enough to know where I am in the book, but not really having read it. In my periphery, I see him pull a straw out of the jar on the counter. He delicately peels off the top few inches of paper, wadding it up and tossing it in the trashcan next to him. He places the straw in his puckered lips, takes a deep breath and blows as hard as he can. The stupid paper wrapper hits me square between the eyes and drops smack into the middle of my book. It takes everything in me not to bust out laughing. I stare down at the white paper nestled in the spine of my book like a makeshift bookmark. I leave it there, marking this moment in time rather than a place in my book. I slide *Honourbound* under the register with care, tucking it under its protective plastic shield before turning back to Khakis.

"Welcome to Beans & Dreams. How can I help you?" I ask in my sweetest fake voice.

"I'm so glad you asked." He's smirking at me, and I hate that I like it. "I'd like to know who painted that mural."

He points to the far wall. People ask about it fairly often. It is so different from Pop's wall of memorabilia and trinkets. But coming from him now, out of the blue, it seems so random. I can't help but feel like he's setting me up to be his punchline and I reflexively stiffen in defense.

"Pablo Picasso," I deadpan. "Michelangelo. Or Raphael maybe? I can't remember. One of the turtles."

He shakes his head and lets out a low chuckle. "No. Seriously, who painted it?"

"Why do you care?" I cross my arms and glare at him.

"Why are you being so evasive?" He crosses his arms to match my pose.

"Because *I* painted it."

Khakis shoots away from the counter like I just waved a steaming turd under his nose.

"Really?" he exclaims in disbelieving shock.

"Yes. Really." I narrow my eyes at him and grit my teeth. He's on dangerous ground if he's going to start talking smack about my artwork. That mural is badass, and he damn well knows it. "First warning." I reach over and pulse the start button on the coffee grinder.

The brief but loud whirling and crunching makes Khakis wince.

"Sorry, no offense intended." He holds up his hands in surrender and takes a few steps back. "For what it's worth, I think it's amazing."

"Oh, good heavens. I can't believe this day has finally come. Khakis likes my painting. I can die a happy woman." I fake swoon and fan myself like a southern belle in the 1800s.

"You're a lot to handle, you know that?" he chides.

I lean across the counter, my tits on display, and eye-fuck the shit out of Khakis while biting my lip. "You have no idea."

He doesn't answer. Instead he blushes slightly and returns to his work.

Another few hours tick by before he finally packs up and makes his way back to the cash register.

"One more question," he starts. His hands are in his pockets, his laptop case slung across his chest. I'll admit, he's kind of cute in a strait-laced, boring sort of way.

I move my hand over to the coffee grinder and nod for him to go on.

"At the risk of my scrotum's safety, can I ask if you're single?"

Damn, I was not expecting that.

"Single as a nun in Antarctica. When your options consist of fuckboys, idiots and assholes, a girl tends to stay single," I answer, desperate to know if he'll have the balls to actually ask me out. Not many guys do. I know I'm a bit *extra*.

"I'm terrified to ask which one of those categories I fall into, but I was wondering if you'd let me buy you a cup of coffee sometime."

"I get my coffee for free," I deadpan.

"Yeah, I guess you would." He gives me a lopsided boyish grin that I admit is mildly adorable. "How about a drink then?"

"Sorry to break it to you, Khakis, but you're so not my type."

He hums and nods, not seeming upset by my rejection. "And what is your type?"

"Not..." I eye him up and down. He's clean-cut and put together. I bet he flosses every night and always refills his ice cube trays, just like a good little robot. "*You*."

I grab a dish tub, cross the shop and start collecting the empty mugs and leftover trash. JC will be here before long and I should try to make the place somewhat presentable.

"That's not an answer."

This kid doesn't quit.

"Believe me, you don't want a real answer." I scrunch up my face and give him my best Jack Nicholson impression. "You can't handle the truth."

"I can handle anything you've got." He's reclining against the edge of his table with a smug little smirk on those pink lips. All manufactured ease and confidence. Now he's a smooth talker?

Nah. I'm done with this game. Time to crush his dreams. I set down the tub and turn to face him full-on. I cock a hip out and prop my hand on it while I gesture to him, up and down several times, with the other.

"Because you're vanilla pudding, and I'm devil's food cake. You're a glass of rosé, and I'm whiskey neat. You're the Gap, and I'm a vintage thrift shop. You're missionary, and I'm kink. You're easy listening, and I'm punk rock."

"That it? That all?" He winks. This fucker actually *winks* at me.

Time to go nuclear. I toss my glasses down on the table with a thud before they skid across the surface. I pull the hair tie out of my ponytail and let my wavy red locks fall past my shoulders. I give it a little tussle, knowing it is barely controlled chaos. *Just like me.* I lick my lips with my eyes locked on his. He's trying hard to keep his composure, but I see him swallow the tension.

"You're too pretty. Too soft. Too clean. Too easy. Too bland. Too safe." I take a slow step towards him with every word. A sexy catwalk strut, crossing my combat-boot clad feet each time, adding an extra sway to my hips. I pin him with a challenging glare as he drinks in my curves with stifled desire.

I lean against him, pressing my chest into his. He doesn't pull away, but his muscles tensed, his body hard. I bring my mouth to his ear.

"I want dirty and dangerous."

Going for the kill, I tease his earlobe with a flick of my tongue. He lets out a deep groan. I shove off his chest and stalk back over to my abandoned dish tub.

I quip over my shoulder, "Darlin', I'd destroy you."

"And I'd enjoy every second of it," he adds without missing a beat.

I bite my lip to keep from smiling.

Chapter Six

Eddie

"You're behind schedule." Instead of a greeting, Darla scolds me without getting up from her desk. The morning sun streaming into her office through the floor-to-ceiling windows behind her and the deceptive clear blue sky almost has me believing that winter is over. The frosty stroll from the subway was enough to prove otherwise. I shake off the chill, unsurprised and undisturbed by Darla's gruffness.

I don't often make the trek downtown to my agent's office. We do most of our meetings by teleconference at my insistence. Crowds are not my thing. Today, Darla refused to do this any way but in person. It was one of the many clues hinting that I am in for a talking-to.

"I am aware," I reply, settling into the couch in the corner rather than the defendant's chair in front of her desk. She's my agent, not my boss. Still, at more than ten years my senior and an industry veteran, she plays the role of pushy older sister quite well. Our relationship is more friendship than business, not that anyone would know it by the scowl on Darla's face right now.

"I don't like it when you're behind schedule."

"I am aware." I lean back, cross my legs and clasp my hands behind my head, not trying to hide my smile.

"Cut the cutesy shit. You miss a deadline and —"

"I know." I interrupt her. "I'm late and I'm out a bunch of money. I've heard this lecture before."

She interlaces her finger, sets her elbows on her desk and leans forward in her plush leather executive chair. She's unsettlingly calm and her voice smooth as ice when she corrects, "*You* miss a deadline and *we're* out a bunch of money."

In addition to a deep respect for Darla, I have a healthy amount of fear of her too. Anyone who has seen her in contract negotiations would. She has no problem giving me a swift boot to the ass when needed. She does it with love. *I think.* It's why after almost ten years and dozens of projects, she's one of the few people still in my life.

I was a young, naive twenty-one-year-old kid when the serious money started rolling in. She could've taken advantage of me, could've manipulated money out of me like my own family did. Could've pretended to like me then used me for the doors I'd open like women have. But instead, Darla watched out for me. Like Benji, she cares about what's best for me despite my pushback. I've never had much of a sense of urgency. A trait that doesn't always mesh well with this industry.

"Have I ever missed a deadline?" I ask incredulously.

"Not yet. Because I've dragged you kicking and screaming across the finish line every damn time."

"I resent that characterization. I'm an artist."

"You're a dog chasing a squirrel."

"I'm a perfectionist."

"You're a pain in my ass."

"But a profitable one."

"Which is the only reason I still put up with you."

"So this has been fun. Same time next month?" I ask with a chuckle and head for the door.

"Get back on schedule!" she shouts at my retreating back.

* * * *

"How was the meeting with Darla?" Benji asks me over his greasy burger and basket of fries.

"Less painful than it could've been," I answer before taking a bite of my own burger.

Benji and I have a standing lunch date at a 1950s-style diner any time I'm downtown. The place is rustic at best, disheveled in a way only Benji would find endearing. He has horrible taste, but I'm a sucker for wedge fries and homemade ice cream.

"She's pissed I'm behind schedule."

"You're always behind schedule." Benji shakes his head.

"You don't rush the creative process." I take a long swallow of my epic vanilla shake.

"Right." He groans. "Did Darla buy that line?"

"Not for a second. But it was worth a try."

"I see you like living dangerously, my friend." Benji smiles, waving a ketchup coated fry in my direction. "What's got you distracted this time?"

"Nothing. I'm not distracted. Why do you both act like I can't ever focus on one task?"

"Because you can't. You get halfway through one project and end up chasing after some new great idea. I love you, man, but you've got a shorter attention span than a Golden Retriever in a ball pit." He smiles up at me, wide and amused. And unaware of the glob of ketchup on his chin. He's picturing the analogy in his head no doubt. Benji has a youthful enthusiasm that never ceases to amaze. I don't think I've ever heard him say a negative word in the years we've known each other.

"That's the second time today I've been referred to as a dog. I'm beginning to take offense."

"If the analogy fits…"

I tug a napkin out of the stainless-steel holder on our table and hand it to Benji.

"You got a little something right there." I tap my chin. He wipes it off, unfazed, before returning to his lunch.

I lean against the booth, the ancient red vinyl groaning in objection under my weight. Staring out the window, I think about the past week. Perhaps I am a little distracted. What I haven't bothered to tell Darla or Benji is that I've been plenty productive, just not on the project they think I should be working on.

I've spent three days in a quirky coffee shop studying a tumultuous woman whose name I don't even know. A woman who made it abundantly clear she has no interest in me. And yet I keep coming back, ravenous for another taste of her sassy attitude and quick wit.

Chapter Seven

Jackie

"Where's Prince Charming?" JC's voice makes me jump right out of my skin.

"Fuck," I shout at him. I snap my glare from the front door to him. "You scared the ever-living shit out of me!"

He holds his hands up in defense. "I wasn't sneakin' around, little Miss Sunshine. I think you're a little distracted."

"Bite me."

"You've been staring at that door for a solid hour, chica. I think someone's got a crush," he teases in an infuriating sing-song voice.

I skirt around him and busy myself with refilling the container of straws, plucking them each individually like it's a field of daisies.

"I love you, JC. But if you think I could ever want to get it on with the human equivalent of a paving stone, you must've been dropped on your head as a child."

"Paving stone?" he asks.

"Stiff, dull and meant to be walked all over."

"*Mentirosa*." He calls me a liar and shakes his head. He stops wiping the counter to snap the towel against my ass with a loud tsk.

"I like messing with him, but that's all it is. He's an easy target."

"You like that he doesn't back down. You know what I call that?"

I lift my chin and cross my arms, waiting on his punchline.

"Foreplay." Jesús bites his lip and winks at me.

"*Foreplay?*" I scoff with a disdainful laugh. "If you think that's foreplay, you're doing it wrong."

"If you don't think foreplay starts long before you get to the bedroom, *you're* doing it wrong." He pouts his lips and cocks an eyebrow. "All that aggressive, teasing banter you two have? The taunting and hinting? Foreplay."

"Oh please. I give everyone shit."

"Not like that. You've never looked at me like you could gobble me up in one sitting."

"Maybe because you're gayer than rainbow sherbet?"

He tilts his head as he squares his shoulders and steps in front of me. "Look me in the eyes and tell me you haven't thought about taking that man upstairs and having your way with him."

I match his stance, squaring my shoulders and staring into his caramel eyes. "I have never and will never fantasize about manicured brown hair, generic gray eyes, average build and pleated khakis."

He blows out a raspberry and saunters off muttering "*mentirosa*" under his breath.

"Tell me, Cupid. If I want to jump his bones so bad, then why did I turn him down when he asked me out?" I lean back against the counter. *Checkmate*.

"He asked you out?" Jesús' eyes twinkle like a housewife watching a Hallmark holiday special.

"For coffee." I gesture around the coffee shop. "Lame."

"You seriously turned him down? Why?"

"Seriously? Earth to Jesús. Are you there?" I shout up to the sky. "You're not listening. He is not my type."

"He may not be your type, but he's the type of guy you *should* be with. Someone who is as smart and sarcastic as you are. Who pushes you. You're just scared of being with a guy who can hold his own."

"Fuck off, JC." I stalk past him, giving his ass a wicked slap with my towel as I do. The loud snap makes me smile. "Scared? I'm not scared of any man. Least of all some mind-numbingly boring and excruciatingly basic upper-middle-class stuffed shirt."

"Mmm-hmmm," JC muses. His chin is tucked down to his chest, his lips pursed and his eyes are narrowed on me. He'd sooner believe I was abducted by aliens. "Whatever you say, chica."

"It doesn't matter anyway. I'd bet my left tit we'll never see him again. Not after I squashed his boyish crush." I shrug.

"Jacqueline Ryan, were you mean to that sweet boy?" JC chides.

"I can't be held responsible for introducing him to the harsh truth. Trust me, I needed to be brutal. I don't want a stray dog following me home."

"Maybe a dog would do you good. Something to soften you up."

"I'm plenty soft," I retort.

JC gestures up and down my body. I'm dressed in all black today, as usual, from my dark eyeliner down to my old boots. My shirt reads *"Despite the look on my face, you're still talking."* It's one of my favorites.

"Darling, I love you. Truly, you're one of my favorite people in the world. But you chase people away with a pitchfork and a snarl."

"Scaredy cats aren't worth my time."

"Not everyone can be a fearless warrior princess. You should give that man a chance."

"Even if I wanted to, it's too late. Trust me, we're never going to see Khakis again."

If I needed any more proof that fate hates me, Khakis chooses that exact minute to barrel into the shop. He's bundled up from head to toe looking like he's wearing an entire L.L. Bean catalog. His cheeks are a rosy pink from the cold, adding to the youthfulness of his soft features. My jaw drops open. Despite the whip of cold air following behind him, my chest heats in an unfamiliar and unnerving sensation.

"You've gotta be fucking kidding me," I groan. JC giggles behind me.

Khakis freezes in the doorway and stares at us, a confused look on his pink, weather-beaten face.

"What?" he asks, completely oblivious.

"Oh nothing. Red just owes me her left tit," JC deadpans.

Chapter Eight

Eddie

My fingers fly across the keys, words flowing like they rarely have in recent months. All on account of my feisty muse. I still haven't gotten her to tell me her name, at least not one I think is real — no one names their little girl Bertha these days. She likes being called Red a bit too much, so I'm working on my own nickname for her.

I keep coming back, despite her rejection and the nearly undrinkable sludge she has the nerve to call coffee. I dump enough sugar in it to cause early onset diabetes, but that's the deal we've silently struck. As long as I pay for a coffee an hour, she'll let me sit at my table in the corner and watch her. *Money well spent.*

I gag on the latest toxic waste in my cup and watch her take the order of some construction worker who looks like he just stepped out of the remake of a Village People music video. Scuffed boots, reflective vest and hard hat tucked under his arm. He's smiling at her like an idiot. *Like I did the first time I saw her.* She smiles back, but it's fake. I've yet to see her really smile, but I know that uninterested look in her eye. I'd put money on her choking back a snarky remark. Sure enough, she gives him her standard *thanks-but-no* grin when his coffee is ready.

I take my empty mug up to the counter and gesture back at the departing construction worker. "Is *that* your type?"

"I don't mind a man with some dirt under his fingernails," she quips without looking at me. She's scrolling through her phone, and I catch a glance at E.B. Jericho's Instagram page. She studies the old cover design posts with focused interest.

"Brawn over brain?" I ask.

"Aren't you a smug little elitist."

I balk. "I'm not an elitist."

"Oh really?" She crosses her arms and leans against the counter. I will myself not to stare at her chest. "You just assume a guy who works construction can't be smart?"

"I didn't mean—"

"Sure you did, Khakis. To you, Bobby must be a high school dropout who's only qualified to work manual labor and crushes beer cans against his empty skull on the weekend. There's no way he could have a master's in mechanical engineering and volunteer at the homeless shelter."

My jaw drops open. "Seriously?"

"Fuck if I know. Never seen him before." She shrugs and stands up straight. Leveling me with her own judgmental gaze, she chastises, "Point is *you* didn't know either."

I shake my head and laugh.

"You've got me there." I hold up my hands in surrender. "Although, you have to admit, a lecture about pre-judging from you is pretty ironic."

"Excuse me?" She cocks an eyebrow and sneers.

I lean against the counter, inching closer to her, and smile at her indignation. "You judged me the second you saw me."

"That's different."

"Oh really?"

"Yeah. First of all, you're basic."

I gasp and grab my chest. "Excuse you."

The hint of a smile ghosts across those scarlet lips before she shakes it off. "And second, I'm better at it."

"Bullshit," I retort, my voice playful but firm.

"How dare you," she chastises and mimics my chest-grab. This sassy, sarcastic woman has me reeling.

"I'll give you a hundred dollars right now if you can tell me what I do for a living." I stare her down, knowing she'll rise to the challenge.

She skirts around the counter and squares up in front of me with a *gimme* gesture. "Let's see the money."

I pull out my wallet, count out five twenties and hold them up.

"Easiest money I've ever made," she quips and reaches for the money.

"Not so fast." I pull it back. "It's a bet. What do I get if I win?"

She tilts her head to the side and purses her lips. "Free coffee for the rest of the day."

"Why would I bet a hundred bucks to win twenty dollars' worth of horrible coffee?"

"Asshole." She crosses her arms. "My coffee is delightful, just like me," she deadpans.

I shake my head and smirk. "Sure you are, Ignis."

"Ignis?"

"You're not the only one who can give someone a nickname." I risk reaching up and tugging on a strand of her red hair. "Latin for fire."

It suits her. Fierce. Independent. Uncontrollable. Intriguing. Dangerous.

"Of course you speak Latin." She swats my hand away and pulls her hair back into a high ponytail. I trail my eyes down the curve of her alabaster neck, imagining the feel of her skin under my lips. I clear my throat and shake the fantasy out of my mind before my imagination gets too carried away.

"That's it." I snap my fingers. "I win, you tell me your name. Your *real* name."

She sighs. "Fine. Deal."

She sticks out a hand, and we shake on it. She circles me slowly, studying me carefully.

"Let's see. You're young but obviously well off since you can spend your mornings sitting around a coffee shop." She grabs my hand and turns it over in her grip. The incidental touch makes my heart race. "Too soft for *real* work."

I don't take the bait.

She drops my hand, and I stretch my fingers to rid them of the tingle her touch caused. Stepping behind me, she trails a finger down between my shoulder blades, and I resist the urge to shudder. *Damn, it's been too long since I've been with someone.*

"I've got it." She circles back, coming to a stop in front of me and staring up with those mischievous eyes.

I steel my features, refusing to give anything away. "Day trader."

A slow smile spreads across my face, and I shake my head. She pouts and spins around with a huff.

"Damn it," she mutters, walking back around the counter.

"Well?" I ask.

"Jackie."

"Jackie…?"

"Jackie Ryan."

"Eddie Jaworski. Pleasure to meet you, Jackie." I hold out my hand, and she shakes it with a low groan that makes me grin like an idiot. Ignis doesn't like losing.

"The pleasure is all yours, I'm sure." She saunters off and makes it a point to ignore me for the rest of the morning. She refuses to come within five feet of me, not even bothering to refill my coffee cup. I return the favor by ignoring her. I keep my eyes focused on my computer screen and force myself to be productive.

"What are you writing?" Jesús asks, startling me.

I was caught up in my work and didn't notice him standing beside my table, fresh coffee in hand. He sets it down in front of me before pulling out a chair and taking a seat. He rests his chin in his hand and studies me.

I look over my screen, not sure what the jumble of words will amount to. "I'm honestly not sure. Not yet."

"How deliciously mysterious," he coos. Shifting in his seat, he glances to the back of the shop where Jackie disappeared about an hour ago, before lowering his voice and asking, "So, what do you think of our little Ms. Jackie?"

I close my laptop and lean against the booth, letting my head drop back against the cushion. I stare up at the ceiling and think about the beautiful enigma that is Jackie Ryan.

"I think she's fascinating."

"Good answer. What are you doing on Tuesday night?"

"I'm flattered, truly." I run my hand down the front of my shirt, smoothing away imaginary wrinkles. "But I'm not—"

"A homosexual?" Jesús' voice is low and sensual. He runs his tongue across his top lip, a slow, languid lick. I clear my throat and sit up. An excruciatingly long silence settles between us, then Jesús bursts out laughing. "No shit, Khakis. No wonder Jackie likes messing with you so much. You're just too easy, sweetheart."

"Thanks," I deadpan. I shove my laptop into my bag.

"But seriously. What are you doing on Tuesday night? Any plans?"

I shake my head and keep putting my stuff away.

"Then you should come out with us."

I stand and take a step toward the door. Jesús twists to watch me go.

"Us?" I ask, turning back, hopeful he means the *us* I think he does.

"Jackie and I never miss amateur night at Bonanza. Best show this side of the Mississippi." He leans forward and shimmies his broad shoulders with a wide smile. He hands me the cell phone from his pocket. "Give me your number. I'll text you the deets."

I punch my number in and hand it back. Making my way to the exit, I pull the door open but still. The question is nagging at the back of my mind.

"Does she know you're inviting me?"

"Where's the fun in that?"

My smile is wide and wily. "I'll be there."

Chapter Nine

Jackie

My pen hovers above the blank page, refusing to make contact. I swirl it around, hoping the flick of my wrist will somehow inspire me and the perfect image will magically appear on the paper. No such luck. It's been fifteen minutes and all I've managed to do is get fifteen minutes older. *Urgh, I sound like my mom.*

I pull up E.B. Jericho's Instagram page. Thirty-five days until my design is due. Disgusted with my lack of progress, I toss the notebook across the room and stalk over to my computer instead. I log in to Rule Them All and take inventory of my empire. I'm richer and more powerful than I was yesterday. I sit up straighter and feel a much-needed sense of pride. Still, I'm never satisfied with yesterday's success. I'm searching for my next conquest when Elizabeth's video chat invite pops up.

"Well, hello there, sexy," I coo into the head piece with an exaggerated eyebrow wiggle.

Elizabeth blushes and shakes her head. The girl's gorgeous inside and out—not that I swing that way—but she doesn't believe it. Austin and I both spend a fair amount of time trying to convince her otherwise. She's smart and sweet. Dedicated and competent. I want to be Elizabeth Wilde when I grow up.

"How are things in Woman'sWorld?" she asks, dodging the compliment.

"Fabulous, just like you. Looking for my next expansion opportunity."

"And in Jackie's world?"

My gaze slides to the open and empty notebook on my floor. That sick sense of failure creeps ups my throat. I swallow it down.

"Slinging coffee and breaking hearts. You know, the usual," I declare, brushing the imaginary chip off my shoulder.

"And drawing?" she prods.

"When the spirit moves me." I shrug. "How's things with Man Meat?"

I spin around in my chair so all she can see is my back, wrap my arms around myself and grope vigorously while making obscene slurping noises. When I turn back around, Elizabeth is blushing again with a stupid happy grin on her face.

I set my elbow on the desk, drop my chin into my hand and lean into the camera. "Tell me, how many orgasms did he give you today?"

"Jackie!" she squeals, and I laugh.

Inquisition successfully dodged. She's so easy to distract that I almost feel bad.

"Austin is good."

I lick my lips. "Yeah, I bet he is."

She rolls her eyes. "What about you? Any prospects?"

"Nah. I'm in a hell of a dry spell. My nethers are woefully under-appreciated these days." The image of Eddie's boyish smile flashes through my mind. *Nope.* He is not the solution to this particular problem. Still, I find myself bringing him up, my mouth seeming to have a mind of its own. "There is this guy at work I kind of like messing with. Khakis."

"Khakis?"

"Yeah." I grin at the stupid nickname that fits him so well. "He's vanilla. Nothing special. *So* not my type." I wave away the completely ridiculous idea.

"Does he work at the cafe too?"

"First of all, it's a coffee shop, not a cafe. I'm a barista, not a waitress."

"Right…"

"There's a difference."

A barista is what entrepreneurs do to make ends meet before they get their first big break. Waiting tables and slinging food is what you do when you're not going anywhere, and you've given up trying.

"Ooookay." Elizabeth isn't trying to be snotty, but she certainly is.

"Whatever. And no, he doesn't work at the *coffee shop*. He is a frequent customer."

"How frequent?" Elizabeth gnaws on her lip, overeager for the sappy details. My bestie is a hopeless romantic.

Over the past week, I can't remember a day Eddie wasn't hunkered down at the same table, either fastidiously working or slyly trying to watch me without getting caught. It's sweet in a weird kind of way.

"Very frequent."

"Sounds like someone's got a crush." Elizabeth simpers.

"Oh, he definitely wants to break himself off a piece of this Jackie pie."

"So, why don't you go for it?"

"Hello? Is this thing on?" I tap the microphone on my computer. "Were you listening? He's not my type."

"Jackie, no offense, but your type is usually assholes. You should go for it. Maybe he could be good for you."

"Urgh. You sound like Jesús. You guys just don't get it. I don't want what's good for me, darling. I want something very, very *bad*. Dirty. Naughty. Downright scandalous. Maybe I'll hire myself a sex tutor too." I wink, teasing her about her ballsy move propositioning Austin when they first met. She looks timid, but Elizabeth is as brave as hell underneath it all, fearless with her heart. *My idol*.

My typically docile friend retorts, "You don't need a sex tutor. You need a life coach to get your act together."

My muscles tense and my blood turns to acid, burning through my veins. I grit my teeth and take a long breath in through my nose to avoid snapping at her. She isn't trying to be harsh, but her words cut deep.

"I'm sorry. I didn't mean—"

"It's fine." My voice is ice cold when I cut her off. "I'm the fuck-up creeping up on thirty and still working at my grandfather's coffee shop, right? Like my mom says, I need to get serious about my future or it will pass me by." I imitate my mom's high-pitched nagging in a failed attempt to lighten the mood.

"Jackie…"

"I better go get my life started. I'll talk to you later." I click off the camera before Elizabeth can say anything else. I know I'm not where I wanted to be, where I thought I would be by now, but I'm a work in progress. I'm biding my time, waiting for the perfect moment to show the world how fucking awesome I am.

Just wait, when I decide to go all out, there won't be anything that can stop me.

I hope.

I spend the rest of the night taking out my anger on internet trolls and gamer assholes. I've dismantled and destroyed a dozen of the most obnoxious players I can find but it doesn't matter. Elizabeth's words are still ringing in the back of my mind as I fall asleep.

Chapter Ten

Eddie

Watch out, world. Jackie Ryan is on the warpath. To the layman, it might look like she's her usual surly self, but I've watched her enough to know there's something more irritating her. Her movements are hard and fast. Jerky with annoyance. The amount of swearing she's doing rivals a construction site. She is slamming dishes a little too hard and muttering a little too often.

We're alone for the first time all morning, so I risk asking, "Everything all right over there?" I slip around the counter to take in all of her.

"Fine!" she screeches, clearly *not* fine.

She's wearing a tight tank top, a shade of deep red like her hair that's up in a messy bun. I trace my eyes over the exposed skin of her shoulders, sweeping down to her ample chest. A neon pink bra pokes out, teasing me with the sight. Baggy dark jeans and a pair of beat-up Converse sneakers completes her casually sexy look.

"I've been told when a woman says she's fine, it means—"

"It means she a fucking adult, and you should mind your own damn business." She stalks over to me, slaps both hands against my chest and gives a hard shove. "Get on your side of the damn counter."

I stumble back a few steps, letting her get her way. Once on the customer side of the counter, I plant my feet so her body slams against mine.

"So pushy," I tease.

She growls. *Literally growls.* A low and violent sound that, weirdly enough, turns me on.

"Watch yourself, Khakis. I'm not in the mood."

She's still using that stupid nickname despite knowing my real name. It annoys me, so I push her, knowing I'm risking bodily harm in the process.

"Because you're so *fine*, Ignis? If you were one of the seven dwarves, you'd be Surly. Like Grumpy but with fewer fucks to give."

I don't get so much as a chuckle. She sidesteps around me, but I reach for her wrist. She snaps her eyes to my hand holding her like a wolf watching a bunny hop right into its den. I drop her arm before she rips mine off.

My mind rambles off a million ways to try and change her mood, to get her out of this funk. Everything from pretending to pull a quarter out of her ear like my Uncle Charlie did to me when I was five to grabbing her and kissing the daylights out of her. *Damn, I want to kiss her.* I shove the idea down. Way. Way. Down. If I tried to kiss her right now, it'd be the last thing I ever did.

"Still think you can guess what I do?"

She gives me a single curt nod.

"Then how about another bet?"

"Terms?"

"Same as last time. You guess what I do, you get a hundred dollars. And if I win, you tell me what's wrong."

She snarls. "I told you I'm *fine*."

I tilt my head and call her bluff. "So you don't want the bet?"

She studies me for a quick moment, weighing her options.

"Sit," she commands, pointing to the empty bench seating at my table. I call it my table because I'm here so often I might as well be paying rent.

I'm a smart enough man to do what I'm told. I'd do just about anything this sexy woman demanded. I fold my hands in my lap and watch her strut up to me, squirming slightly in my seat.

With a hand on each shoulder, she leans over me. Even more of that pink bra slips out from underneath her tank top. I lick my lips and try not to leer at her amazing breasts.

"I get three guesses this time."

I clear my throat and I shake my head. "That wasn't the deal."

"If you're too scared to take the bet…"

She leans back, but I slip a hand around her leg to keep her from stepping away. Her supple thigh tenses under my touch. Her skin is hot beneath her jeans. My mouth goes dry and my heartbeat drums against my skull.

"I'm not scared of you, Ignis." My voice is low, but sharp. She hears me. A naughty grin twists on those perfect ruby lips.

"Good. Then you'll be more fun to break." She flicks the collar to my light blue dress shirt before smoothing it down again. She rolls her neck like she's preparing for a brawl. "All right. Let's do this."

I let my hand slide off her leg and land back in my lap before tilting my chin at her. *Your move.*

"Architect."

I shake my head. She purses her lips.

"I knew it. Too creative."

I lock down my laugh, refusing to give away any free hints. Jackie gnaws at her bottom lip, ruining the scarlet lipstick she wears every day. The one that does very dangerous things to my private thoughts.

"Computer programmer?"

Slowly, I shake my head. I could swear I hear the lightning strike when she perks up.

"Ooooh. You're going down. I've got it." She smirks and it's sexy as hell. Angry. Sassy. Smug. This woman is irresistible, no matter her mood. "Accountant."

I hang my head and slouch my shoulders, defeated.

"I knew it!" she crows, dancing around the cafe with an intoxicating sway of those curvy hips. With the joy radiating off her, I almost wish I were an accountant. She spins, points at me and shouts, "Suck it, Khakis!"

"I can't believe...you think I'm an accountant," I drawl.

She freezes, her arms dropping to her side like dead weight. "You're not?" she asks like a kid told Santa doesn't exist.

"Not. Even. Close."

She grabs a cellophane-wrapped muffin off the counter and throws it at my head. "You're such an asshole!"

I catch the baked projectile and laugh. She's not mad. Not really. Not like she was ten minutes ago. I'll call that a success. I unwrap the muffin and take a big bite. Blueberry's never been my favorite, but damn if this isn't the sweetest muffin I've ever tasted.

"You going to pay up?" I pat the bench next to me.

She blows a hard breath out her nose, but stomps over nonetheless and sits.

"What has you feeling so *fine* today?" I ask.

She flails her hands around in big circles. "My best friend said something that pissed me off. That's it. Not a big deal."

"What'd they say?"

"It doesn't matter."

"A bet is a bet, Ms. Ryan."

Jackie moans like she's in pain, not happy about having to tell me what's wrong.

"Urgh. You are so annoying." She fidgets with her tank top, adjusting the strap while she shifts awkwardly in her seat. I mourn the loss of her beautiful chest but am silently thankful it will be easier to pay attention to her words.

Her voice is soft when she finally says, "She told me I need a life coach."

That's not exactly what I was expecting. Jackie is a force of nature. An impenetrable fortress of attitude and arrogance. Then it hits me. *It's an act.* The confidence. The brash, too-cool-for-school attitude is a front. Underneath all of that, Jackie is just as scared as the rest of us. And right now, she's letting me see it.

"Why did that upset you so much?" I've never been so fascinated with another human being. I want to crawl inside her mind and know every inch of her. Her pain. Her pleasure. Her dreams. Her fears. The good, bad and indifferent. I want it all.

"Because I don't!" she shouts. "I'm doing fine. She keeps bugging me about this stupid design competition, and I don't need it. I've already got one nagging mother, and believe me, that is enough."

Jackie shoots up and paces back and forth in the small space between the tables.

"She has no idea how hard it is to come up with a completely original cover design."

My mind screeches to a stop and goes blank. A tightness forms in the center of my chest, a deep and resounding panic.

"Cover design?" I ask cautiously, my voice cracking.

Jackie snatches a towel from beside the register and absentmindedly wipes the same six inches of the counter.

"There's this contest… It's not a big deal…" Jackie's soft voice trails off. She stares blankly out of the shop window. "Every time there's a new E.B. Jericho release, they hold a cover contest. You submit a design and if you win, it's the cover of the next book."

My palms get sweaty. I feel like I'm sitting under a heat lamp. My whole body catches fire. The tightness squeezes harder, and I can't breathe.

"E.B. Jericho?" I ask reflexively. Panic is keeping me from being able to think clearly. Of course I knew she was a fan, but her entering the contest is different. Things are getting a bit too complicated.

Jackie rolls her eyes at me. "She's a sci-fi writer. *The* sci-fi writer. And this is the last book in her *Sins of Tomorrow* series, so it's a huge deal."

I smile, wide and toothy, like an absolute idiot. "I know who E.B. Jericho is. Actually —" The words are on the tip of my tongue when she interrupts.

"Sure you do," Jackie scoffs in disbelief.

"Read every book."

"Bullshit. Name one," she challenges.

I point to the mural behind me. "*Honourbound.*"

"How'd you know that?" Jackie's jaw drops open, and her eyes go wide.

I shrug. "Pretty obvious. It's exactly how I pictured it." A moment of silence passes between us before I add, "I told you I thought it was awesome."

She nods. And blushes. *Blushes.* Jackie Ryan can blush. Who knew?

Chapter Eleven

Jackie

I jog in place, trying to keep from freezing to death. I forgot my scarf and I don't even own a pair of gloves. People like my mom shop for gloves. Adults who care about the thread count in their sheets and buy organic fruit. I'm a pockets kind of girl. Well, technically I own red satin gloves that go with the devil costume I wore last Halloween. Flexing my numb fingers, I wish I'd thought to wear them. They'd to be better than nothing.

Under my jacket I'm only wearing a Misfits crop-top T-shirt, a leather miniskirt and fishnet stockings. I look sexy as hell, but I'm about to get frostbite in very unpleasant places. It can't be more than twenty degrees out tonight. The sky is clear, but it feels like it should be snowing. There is an icy bite to the air, like it's angry at the world and all the people foolish enough to be out in it. I'm chilled down to my bones and ready for a nip of something to get the blood flowing back into my toes.

"What are we waiting for, JC? I'm freezing and I need a margarita like, yesterday."

"Five more minutes. I'm meeting a friend," he answers. He stands up on his tippy-toes as if that's going to make the difference as he peers down the crowded street.

"A friend?" I'm instantly livid. "How could you? Bonanza is our thing."

"Calm down, little Ms. Thing. He's just a friend."

"Bullshit. I'm going home. I'm not going to be the third wheel to one of your Grindr hook-ups." I stomp my feet and pout, but don't actually leave. I'm all dressed up and I'll be damned if I'm going home sober.

"You are the biggest drama queen I have ever met. He is just a friend. He doesn't swing my way, trust me."

"I can't bel –" My words get stuck in the back of my throat when I glance over JC's shoulder and meet a familiar pair of blue-gray eyes. "What the actual fuck?" I manage to stutter.

The crowd fades and my attention is locked on Eddie. He looks like a Macy's catalog model, pleasantly non-threatening. He's wearing a slim-fit, camel-colored peacoat with a dark green scarf poking out at his chest. His hair is slicked back, and his cheeks are a rosy pink that matches those lips that are curled up into a teasing smile. He's amused as hell to have caught me off guard. He steps through the mass of bodies with a practiced ease, looking very posh and out of place.

"Good evening, Jesús." He holds out his hand, and JC shakes it. "Jackie." He adds my name as an afterthought, like he doesn't care if I'm here or not. *Mentiroso.*

A guy with rusty-colored hair and dark green eyes sidles up next to Eddie with a wide and friendly smile.

"Hey, guys," he calls out like he knows us. I don't give him more than a sideways glance. I'm too busy pinning Eddie to the sidewalk with a glare.

"Can I introduce my friend, Benjamin Kelly?" Eddie says before stepping aside.

"Ben," the guy adds, shaking JC's hand. "Thanks for letting me crash your evening. When Eddie told me where he was going tonight, I couldn't help but invite myself along. This place is supposed to have the best margaritas in the state. I've been trying to get this guy to come out here with me for weeks, but you know how he is." He smacks Eddie on the shoulder with a loud thwack.

"Khakis isn't much for adventure." I simper.

"Khakis?" Ben asks, covering a laugh by pretending to cough into his hand. Eddie levels him with a cutting look. "Well, shall we?"

Ben holds his arm out to Jesús who takes it with a sly smile and a soft blush. He's such a romantic sap. I make a mental note to threaten Ben's manhood if he hurts JC.

"And what exactly do you think you are doing here?" I ask, stepping in front of Eddie and blocking his way into the theater. The bitter cold is a distant memory with the fire raging through my veins.

"I was invited." He sidesteps, but I shift in front of him again.

"Not by me." My tone is flat. I try and hide my amusement behind indifference.

"Amazingly enough, you aren't the center of my universe." He tilts his head and juts out his dimpled chin. His challenge makes my heart rate kick up a notch.

I dance my fingers up the buttons of his jacket and wrap my hand around his soft, warm scarf. His hands are in his pockets, undisturbed by my taunting which makes me want to push him further. He tilts his head and watches the fog of our warm breaths. Rising like smoke from a dragon's mouth, it mingles together in the small space between our bodies. He stares at me like I'm some mystical creature, bizarre and mesmerizing.

With a fistful of cashmere, I quip, "A drag show isn't your bag, Khakis. Don't you have a garden party to attend?"

He reaches up and pries my frozen fingers off his scarf. His hands are so warm, my skin sizzles at his touch. He narrows his eyes on my curled fingers. He takes my other hand, clasps them together in front of us, and rubs them like he's trying to start a fire with the friction. I'd pull away if his touch didn't feel absolutely amazing.

"There's a lot you don't know about me, Ignis," he says, staring at our steepled hands.

My hands begin to thaw with his touch, and his movement slows to a soft caress before finally stopping. He peers over our joined hands and those penetrating eyes find mine. The bustle of the street is the dull buzz of a beehive, faded and indistinguishable.

"What I wouldn't give for a coffee grinder right now," I tease to break the weighty silence. Pulling my hands out of his, I turn and walk away, ignoring the way my heart is pounding and the smile that's getting harder to suppress.

It is impossible not to be in a good mood inside Bonanza. Queen Mab, the emcee, is the most enthusiastic person I've ever met, and her energy is contagious. She is over six foot in her heels. A tall drink of joy in a full-length lime-green sequin ball gown. Her makeup is on point, thick black eyeliner in a sexy cat-eye, deep red blush highlighting her high cheekbones and shimmering just-been-licked lips. She's more woman than I'll ever be, and I love it.

"Who's ready to have some fun?" Queen Mab calls out to the audience, her arms spread as wide as her megawatt smile. JC, Ben and I all hoot and holler. Eddie claps like he's at a golf tournament.

JC and I usually grab a table close to the stage, but we've upgraded to one of the crushed red velvet horseshoe-shaped booths tonight to fit the four of us. I think Ben and JC spent the few minutes Eddie and I were outside plotting the seating arrangements to make sure we were crammed next to each other. Ben is on Eddie's left and JC is on my right. They keep leaning across the table, pretending like it's so loud they need us to scrunch up as much as possible. Eddie's arm is on the booth behind me to let me get closer, and I'm all but sitting in his lap.

Queen Mab is not satisfied. "Oh, I know you can do better than that. Come on. Who wants to have some fun tonight?"

The crowd gets louder, the four of us along with it.

"I can't hear you!" Queen Mab shouts back.

I scream my head off. JC cups his hands around his mouth and shouts. Even Ben lets out the loudest whistle I've ever heard. Finally, Eddie gets into it. I hear him let out a woot beside me and I crack a smile. It is going to be fun shoving him right out of his comfort zone tonight.

Queen Mab is three songs into her set when I polish off my first margarita.

"Can I get you another?" Eddie asks. He leans in, his nose brushing against the crest of my ear. The ghosting touch is surprisingly erotic.

I answer him with a single quick nod, handing him my empty margarita glass. Eddie turns to Ben and motions for him to get out of the booth. He doesn't.

"Shots?" Ben asks, pointing across the table to JC.

"Shots!" JC squeals and downs his margarita. The pair turn to me, eyes dancing with excitement.

"Shots?" they ask in unison.

"Shots." I give the only correct answer.

"Shots?" The three of us turn to Eddie.

"*No* shots," he answers. Ben shrugs and scoots out of the booth. JC is quick on his heels, a fist pumping in the air in time to the beat of Queen Mab's rendition of *Barbie Girl*.

"Benji! Seriously, no shots." Eddie's objection dies in the noise of the bar.

The two of us are alone in the dimly lit booth. I don't pull away, despite having the room to now. Instead, I lean into him, feeling the way he shifts against me, like he's not sure if he wants more or less contact. It's a fun game of silent torture.

Ben and JC come back with a bottle of tequila, limes and salt. And four glasses. They slide back into the booth all giggles and conspiratorial smiles. JC sets a glass down in front of each of us, and Ben pours four shots. Eddie's head drops back against the booth with a thud.

"What's wrong, Khakis? Don't know how to take a shot?" I tease. When Eddie looks over at me, I take a long slow lick of my wrist. He shifts in the booth to watch me. I maintain eye contact. *Lick. Salt. Lick. Shot.*

Suck. I smack my lips and simper at him. "It's easy. You just relax your throat and swallow."

"Fine," Eddie groans, downing his shot in a single quick motion. No chaser. It's quality tequila, but I expect him to grimace or cough. Nope. He's smooth as silk. My mouth drops open. "What?"

"You're right," I confess.

"Of course I am," he declares definitely, before adding, "About what?"

"There's a lot I don't know about you."

We clink our glasses and take our second shots. The liquid heat pumps through my body and makes me curl my toes in my steel-toed boots. My cheeks are on fire. I want to shiver and shake out the overwhelming sensation, but I refuse to let Khakis see me off my game.

"All right, my precious ones. It's Tuesday and here at Bonanza that can only mean one thing," Queen Mab calls out to the crowd. "We need some fresh meat for you to devour because it's…amateur night!"

The crowd goes wild, screaming and clapping. Queen Mab makes her way off the stage, helped ever so delicately by two muscly men in nothing but cuffs on their wrists, red banana hammocks and bowties. She kisses each on the cheek before sashaying out into the audience. The spotlight follows her, hitting every sequin on her dress and making her a human disco ball.

"Do you all know how this goes?" she asks the crowd in general. She stops in front of a table with a man and woman who I'm guessing are on their third date. They like each other, but they're far from comfortable. They're still in what I call the lie-your-ass-off stage, trying to put that best foot forward and lock down a life partner before they know all each other's nasty habits.

Queen Mab grabs the guy's shoulder and squeezes. "How about you, sexy? Do you know how this goes?" He shakes his head with an awkward smile. Queen Mab shoots up and covers her dramatic gasp with her hand.

"He's a virgin," she whispers into the microphone before adding, "Yummy. For this sexy slice of man right here and all you other Bonanza virgins out there, this is how it works. We round up six volunteers from you amazing people out here in the audience. We turn you over to the impeccable stylings of Lita, Gita and Anita." Queen Mab motions up to the stage where her three helpers are each decked out in their own neon ball gown with matching hair.

"They will turn you into the most fab-YOU-lous drag princesses ever. And once your transformation is complete, you will strut your sexy new look up on stage while singing your heart out. The drag princess who captures the most hearts will be proclaimed Her Royal Highness, Queen of the Night. She gets this sparkly crown to show everyone she's fine, fierce and foxy. Plus, she'll also get this bottle of bubbly to share with whoever she so chooses and most importantly, bragging rights!"

Queen Mab throws her arms up and the crowd cheers. There's an excited charge in the room, a no-stress-allowed vibe as if the outside world can't touch us. For a few hours, it's margaritas, music and laughs. A grown-up playground with no adulting required. I love it here.

"So who out there has a burning desire that only thigh-highs and hairspray can quench? Do we have six brave souls out there tonight just waiting for their chance to be…pretty woman walkin' down the street?"

She sings the last few words in her soulful voice, the cheap pink tiara prize twirling on her finger.

"Ouch!" Eddie screams and shoots up out of the booth. He's rubbing his back and wincing, looking around for what I'm assuming was Ben's salad fork in his ass cheek. Before Eddie can sit back down, the spotlight swings over to him. He stands there, completely frozen, like that rat on my kitchen floor when I surprised it at two a.m. looking for a midnight Twinkie. His mouth drops open, and his eyes go wide.

Ben jumps up and slings and arm over his shoulders shouting, "Hell yeah, Eddie. I'm right there with you. We're in!"

"What? I wasn't—"

Never to be outdone, JC jumps up next and shouts, "You're going down, bitches. That crown is mine." JC and I come to Bonanza so much that he's more semi-pro than amateur.

Before the somewhat drunk and very uncomfortable Eddie can form a real argument, all three of my men are swept backstage for their makeovers along with the third-date guy and two other eager volunteers.

Me? I try to take another shot of tequila but can't stop laughing long enough to pour. My whole body is shaking with the giggles. I could live a million lifetimes and never forget the look of utter shock and horror on Eddie's face. It will keep me warm on many long, lonely nights to come.

While the guys are gone getting prettied up, I do my daily scroll through Instagram and Reddit. The Rule Them All sub-Reddit is abuzz with rumors of major changes to gameplay. This happens every few months. Some people in the game don't have enough skill—or balls—to be successful, so they start rumors about how this or that is going to change just to distract everyone while they make a land grab or pump up demand for their exports. It's always bullshit. This time it's talk about the whole game shutting down. *Fuck off*. There's no way in hell. Rule Them All isn't going anywhere, and neither is Woman'sWorld.

Queen Mab finishes her set with a rendition of *Vogue* to a round of enthusiastic applause before introducing the new and improved drag princesses. JC is up first. He's rocking a curly auburn wig, a leopard print pantsuit and black stilettos. Honestly, it's toned down compared to some of his regular club attire. Before the music even starts, I know he's going to sing *Wind Beneath My Wings*. It's his absolute favorite karaoke song. He loves to raise his hand on the high notes like he's testifying. I don't know about drag princess, but he's one hell of a drama queen.

Ben is up next. I don't know if it was his choice, or his stylist's, but his "new look" is straight-up slutty. He's in a black leather bustier, a red boa and matching red platform heels. The confident stride he has out to the middle of the stage confirms it's not his first time navigating in women's footwear. The lights dim and an excited hush falls over the crowd. Just when I think Ben has succumbed to stage fright, his confident tenor rings out.

"It's Britney, bitch."

The lights come up and the crowd is on their feet. Ben brings the house down with his version of *Gimme More*. There are hip thrusts, chest shimmies and yes, even some twerking. That boy can move.

Now it is Khaki's turn. Poor, poor, Eddie.

He stumbles out on stage, off balance physically and emotionally. He's covered head-to-toe in an emerald-green chiffon dress that reminds me of the one my mom tried and failed to get me to wear to my junior prom. He stands up straight, his broad shoulders back and his eyes closed. He doesn't sing *Can't Take My Eyes Off Of You* so much as recite it. It's like bad spoken-word poetry. A stalker's pledge.

The crowd at Bonanza is unwaveringly enthusiastic, but even they are lukewarm in their support for poor Eddie. After Ben got the whole audience worked up, Eddie came in with a fizzle. I feel a little bad for him. Maybe that's why I decided to join in, I can't help rooting for the underdog.

I jump up on our table littered with shot glasses and sing at the top of my lungs, "Oh, pretty baby!"

The spotlight finds me, and half the audience turns around to look. I stomp my foot in time with the beat and everyone starts clapping along. My heart is racing, and I can't keep a stupid smile off my face. It's not from the hundred pairs of eyes on me, but the single pair up on stage that are twinkling with relief and thankfulness.

Eddie and I lock eyes across the room and sing to each other like we're fighting. Like we're angry and happy at the same time. Like we drive each other crazy, and we can't get enough.

When the music stops, the applause snaps me back into the moment. I give a quick curtsy and climb down off the table with the help of Queen Mab's half-naked stagehands. When the spotlight fades, I sneak a couple of glances back up to Eddie on the stage. Each time, I can tell he's searching for my face in the darkness. It fills my chest with a giddy power, like the moon changing the tide.

Ben wins the crown, rightfully so, but Eddie and "his unnamed accomplice" get an honorable mention. Settled back in at our table, Ben and JC are on one side of the booth, sharing the victory champagne and arguing about who wore it better. The three are in their regular clothes again but had varying success with getting their makeup off. I have a feeling Ben will be finding glitter in unusual places for the next month.

Eddie drapes an arm along the booth behind me and leans in to whisper, "Thank you."

I brush him off. "You were just too pathetic up there. You were bringing the whole place down."

He nods and pulls his arm back. He's staring into his drink with that hard look he gets sometimes when he's focused on his laptop in the coffee shop.

"I told you this wasn't your scene." I elbow him in the side. "It takes a real man to rock fishnets."

He chuckles half-heartedly. "It's not the fishnets that scare me." He downs another shot of tequila without so much as a wince. "It's being in the spotlight. I hate having so many people looking at me. It makes me feel like I can't breathe."

"I get that," I confess. Without thinking, I place my hand just above his knee and squeeze. I do get it. My attitude is my armor. His clothes are his camouflage. We're both just trying to survive.

"You do?" he asks, staring at my hand.

"Judgment is a bitch."

He turns his head, and I catch that boyish grin of his. Much to my horror, it makes me smile too. My gaze drifts up to those soft eyes, and I feel myself leaning into him. We're having what saps like Jesús call "a moment". A wave of claustrophobic panic washes over me. I'm trapped. Not by the cramped space or the loud noise, but by his genuine admiration and the spark it lights deep inside of me.

"Fuck, I'm so wasted," I mutter with an exaggerated hiccup before burying my face in Eddie's chest.

Chapter Twelve

Eddie

"You look nice today," I compliment Jackie while handing her a twenty for my daily coffee tab.

"And normally I look like what exactly?" Her tone is distant, not her usual playful teasing. She walks away, leaving me with the distinct impression I've done something wrong. I push down the urge to ask her what. She wouldn't give me a straight answer anyway. I press on, undeterred by her cold shoulder.

"You're alluring every day but being pissed off gives you that special hostile glow." I lean against the counter and grin at her. She pinches her eyes shut and shakes her head, fighting back a smile. *Victory.* She fills a coffee mug with my caffeinated sludge and struts back over.

"Walk away before you dig a hole you can't climb out of, Khakis." She slides the mug in front of me and crosses her arms.

"Sure thing, Ignis." I take a long sip of my coffee and keep my eyes locked on hers. She groans and shoos me away. I keep the eye contact with a lopsided grin as I walk backward to my table. She likes me and she knows it, even if she refuses to admit it.

I'm settled in with my makeshift desk set up, laptop and notebook at the ready about fifteen minutes later. I'm about to dig in and get to work when Jackie's light laugh rings out in the coffee shop. I lift my eyes to find a hipster leaning up against the counter. *He can't be her type.* He has a long, manicured beard and a man bun poking out the bottom of his fedora. He's wearing tight, short slacks that on a woman would be called capris and a long scarf draped over his designer distressed-cotton T-shirt. My mouth drops open, my eyes go wide and my fists clench at my sides when I see her slide a piece of paper across the counter to him. Her number no doubt.

"Oh come on!" I groan, loud enough they hear me. The hipster ignores me, but Jackie stares daggers that make me fear for my personal safety.

"Thanks," Hipster says, slipping the piece of paper with Jackie's number into his skin-tight pocket before giving her a quick nod and hitting the road.

I try to re-focus on my work, but Jackie has other ideas. She stalks up to my table and slams down a new cup of coffee. It sloshes over the sides, and I snatch my notebook to keep it from soaking up the dark roast.

"You have something to say, Professor Cockblock?" she snarls.

"You can't be serious. That guy?" I gesture with my thumb toward the door and tsk.

She shrugs. "The pussy wants what it wants."

"And what could it *possibly* want from that guy? Man-scaping tips?"

She pulls out the chair next to me and sits down with her elbows on the table, her face in her hands. In her taunting sing-song voice she tells me, "Well, sweetie. When two grown-ups like each other very, very much…" Her tone turns naughty. "They take a scenic trip to pound town."

"You know, I've been meaning to travel more. Care to show me the sights?"

She pulls that full blood-red bottom lip into her mouth and bites back a smile. "Oh, honey, you need to take the training wheels off before you can go mountain biking." She pats the top of my hand and saunters off.

I follow right behind her. She's leaning over a table, wiping it down when I sidle up. "Maybe you're just a tease," I lean down and murmur into her ear.

"Ha!" Jackie barks out a laugh. She straightens and spins around to face me. She sucks in a quick breath, probably with the realization of how close we are but recovers quickly and hardens her features. We aren't touching, but our bodies are as close as they can get without being wrapped around each other. The tension is pulling me into her like a magnet.

"Pah-lease. Don't get pissy because I need a man who knows there's more to life than missionary. I told you, Khakis, you're not my type."

"First of all, my name is Eddie." I tower over her. My voice is firm with my growing annoyance. I'm tired of this woman brushing me off when we both feel the simmering attraction between us. A spark of heat flashes in her eyes and sends my heart racing. Fighting with her is the best kind of excitement. "Secondly, I call bullshit. You think *I'm* vanilla? That guy was a walking cliché. I bet he hasn't had an original thought in his entire life."

"First of all, he's hot. I don't care if he's stupid, so long as he's not *boring*." She says it like it's the ultimate crime. She leans forward, pressing her perky tits into me and making me lose my train of thought momentarily. She lowers her voice to a wicked challenge. "And secondly, check yourself before you wreck yourself, *Eddie*. The coffee grinder is ready for its next victim."

I ignore her threat, knowing it's her go-to defense mechanism. "Boring? You think I'm boring?" I place my hands on the table behind her, pinning her against it and pressing our bodies together, not allowing a sliver of space for her to escape this time.

"Yes. You, Eddie Jaworski, are B-O-R-I-N-G. Boring." Her voice is soft and sugary, like she's whispering sweet nothings to me. I've never been so turned on by being insulted. "You dress like Old Navy threw up," she purrs.

"And you, Jackie Ryan, dress like a colorblind five-year-old." I tuck a strand of bright red hair behind her ear and cup her face. Her eyes find mine and they're full of amused surprise. I drop my gaze to her beautiful lips. I close my eyes and hold my breath as I lean in for the kiss I've been craving since the day I met her.

Just before our lips meet, she sucks in a sudden surprised gasp and shoves me back with both hands.

"Nice try, Khakis," Jackie teases with a warm laugh. Her voice is high-pitched and shaky. She slips away and retreats behind the counter. She's trying to hide it, but her breath is coming quick, and I bet her heart is racing just like mine.

"So what, you won't fuck anyone with an IRA?" I ask, with a sharp tinge. I sit on the edge of the table and cross my arms. My gaze follows her as she putters around behind the counter.

"Shocking, isn't it? Hard to fathom that financial stability doesn't get me wet," she quips.

"You do realize being mature doesn't have to mean being boring? You can have full dental *and* enjoy a little kink."

She dips her head and slouches her shoulders forward. A loud, rattling snore echoes across the coffee shop before she snaps back up. She shakes her head and blinks her eyes with an exaggerated stretch and yawn.

"I'm sorry, I dozed off there for a second. What were you saying?" She gives me that condescending smirk that makes my blood boil.

What I wouldn't give to bend her over my knee and give her the spanking she deserves.

Chapter Thirteen

Jackie

"You're up!" Pops is clearly surprised to find me getting ready for work at the ass-crack of dawn.

"Yeah, yeah, yeah. I'm up," I groan as I apply a second coat of mascara to finish off my sexy cat-eye. I'm sitting cross-legged on the floor in front of my full-length mirror. It's precariously leaning against my closet door since I never got around to hanging it on the wall. I took the shade off my desk lamp for extra light since the ceiling light burned out last month and I haven't replaced it. Adulting isn't my strong suit.

"And to what does the world owe this rare pleasure?" Pops asks. He lets out an old-man groan when he lowers himself onto my unmade bed to watch me. He probably hasn't been keeping on top of his arthritis medicine. I bite back the urge to scold him. I'm in no place to judge.

"Nothing. I just woke up early."

Pops hums in disbelief. "It couldn't have anything to do with that handsome young man Jesús introduced me to?"

"Khakis? No way. He's not my type, Pops."

"Who cares about your type? That boy is a young Gene Kelly. If I were fifty years younger, I could teach him a few things."

"Pops! Ewww. Overshare."

"Oh please, don't pretend you haven't imagined taking advantage of that young man."

"Maybe," I admit with a devious smile. "He is fun to mess with."

"Mess with? Is that what the kids are calling it these days?"

"No, you dirty old bastard." I swat his thigh. "I mean he's fun to tease. And he doesn't back down. Which is kind of sexy, I guess. But we're total opposites." I shake my head and wave off the idea.

"Opposites attract for a reason, sweetest."

With an annoyed groan, I stand up and pull a cropped leather jacket out of my closet. "Why is everyone so obsessed with the idea of me hooking up with the human embodiment of an after-school special?"

"Maybe we all want to see you happy."

"I *am* happy," I growl. "And you sound like Mom."

"Your mother can be demanding, but she is also full of so much love."

My mood instantly sours. "Don't start, old man."

"She loves you more than life itself. Don't lose sight of that."

"Sure she does." My words are soaked in sarcasm and derision.

"Jackie…" Pops uses his warning tone.

"I know she loves me, all right?" I snap. "Why do you think her disappointment hurts so bad? I can only take her *love* in small doses, parsed out. A little bit of guilt-tripping goes a long way you know!"

Anxiety and shame bubble up in my chest. I'm not the daughter she wants. I'm not polished or successful. Not put-together and accomplished. Not her. Every conversation we have always starts with how I am not enough.

"She wants what's best for you. She pushes because she believes in you."

"Ha! She believes in my ability to screw up and fall short of her expectations. Besides, you're one to talk." I circle my hand in the air and gesture to all of Pops. From the pomade in his hair, to his partially unbuttoned peach shirt, the sparkle of his gold necklace and the mirror shine on his dress shoes, he looks like the caricature of a dapper nineteen-fifties porn star. He has his own style, marches to the beat of his own drum and for that he's always been my idol. Pops is who he is. No apologies given. No forgiveness needed. That doesn't sit well with Mom's cookie-cutter idea of life.

"Even the best of us have our demons. I decided a long time ago that I'd earned the right to grow old disgracefully. Your mother hasn't forgiven me for that just yet. But that doesn't mean we don't love each other."

"So it's okay for you two to love each other and not talk? Sounds great. Where do I sign up?" Snark drips from my sarcastic words. I'm not a morning person and this chat with Pops is making me remember why mornings can bite the fattest part of my ass. I stomp around my tiny studio apartment, frustration making my skin burn. "I'm going to be late to work."

"Good thing I know the owner."

I walk to my open door, ignoring him.

"Jackie—"

"What?" I spin on my heels, cross my arms and level my grandfather with a glare. *It's too early for this.*

Pops stands up and walks toward me.

"I didn't mean to pick a fight, sweetest. You know I love you." He holds out his arms for a hug, and I give in. My temper flares quickly, but I've never been able to hold on to my anger for long, especially with Pops.

"Do an old man a favor?" He cups my cheek and kisses my forehead. "Call your mother. And remember her nagging comes from a place of love."

"You sure I can't just give you a kidney or something?" I deadpan.

"Afraid I'm all set in the organ department."

"Damn it."

Chapter Fourteen

Jackie

My phone vibrates in my pockets, and I ignore it. Ethan, AKA the hipster, has texted a handful of times over the past few days since I gave him my number. I've ignored all of them. I threw up in my mouth a little when he invited me to *'take a stroll'* around the farmer's market. *Really, dude?* I'll never admit it to Eddie, but he is right. Hipster cliché is not my type. From his patchouli-scented beard down to his intentionally distressed leather boots, he is basic with a capital B.

I was never really interested in him. Sure, he'd be fun to ironically hang out with a few times. Get some good laughs with Elizabeth at his expense and maybe a few orgasms if I'm lucky, but three dates tops and his whole thing would get old. I get bored quickly and mocking a clueless hipster is too easy. At least Eddie knows when I'm mocking him and rises to the occasion.

Ethan wouldn't know a double entendre from double penetration.

If I'm honest, the only reason I gave him my number was to see how Eddie would react. And he didn't disappoint. His little temper tantrum was more fun than any stroll around a pretentious organic market could ever be. It's as hot as hell when he gets all assertive. For a minute, he had me wondering if there is more to him than his khakis and his IRA.

I look up across the coffee shop to find him sitting at his same seat, hunkered down with his notebook and laptop all set up just so. He is painfully predictable. It's cute, in a vanilla sort of way. I still don't know what he does for a living. I'm starting to wonder if he has a job at all. Maybe he's like Elizabeth, a trust-fund baby whose family has more money than God.

My phone vibrates in my pocket again, and I finally decide to break the hipster's heart. He'll have to solo the farmer's market. Silver lining, more organic figs for him. To my surprise, it's not him that's been blowing up my phone. It's Elizabeth.

Lizbit: Have you heard? Are you okay?
Lizbit: Jackie?!? Hello?
Lizbit: If you haven't heard, DO NOT check your email. I'm serious!
Lizbit: Call me as soon as you get this.
Lizbit: JACQUELINE RYAN, please tell me you haven't done anything crazy...

What the hell is she going on about? For once, I do as I'm asked and call her without checking my email.

"What's up, crazy pants?" I ask as soon as she answers. "Quintuple text much?"

"Jackie. Thank God! I've been so worried about you." Elizabeth's voice is shaky, and the first licks of panic gnaw at the corner of my mind.

"You're freaking me out, Lizbit." I'm louder than I should be, my words carrying through the shop and drawing attention from Eddie and the few other customers we have this morning. I lower my voice and ask, "What's going on?"

"I want you to take a deep breath."

"Elizabeth…" I groan, annoyed and exasperated.

"Okay, fine. I'm just going to rip it off like a Band-Aid…"

I'm waiting on pins and needles for her next words, but instead there's just silence. "Elizabeth!" I shout. Every set of eyes in the shop turns to me in alarm.

"Legendary Games is discontinuing support for Rule Them All. They're killing our game."

NO! I scream inside my head. I'm in shock. I can't form any actual words. *It can't happen.* I've been playing Rule Them All for a decade. I can't count how many hours I've spent shaping Woman'sWorld, building partnerships and demolishing my foes. It is like home. My safe space. Acceptance. It's where I met Elizabeth, for fuck's sake. *They can't take that away.*

"There has to be a mistake," I mumble into the phone.

"You have a notification in your email. That's why I didn't want you looking at it."

"It must be a joke. Some kind of fucked-up prank."

Elizabeth's tone is soft and cajoling, like she's talking to a crazy person with their finger on a hair-trigger. *Not too far off.* "I wish it were. I've double- and triple-checked. The company has stopped all planned upgrades with full server support to cease in six months."

"*No!*" I howl.

"Jackie, are you okay?" I'm too lost to notice Eddie is out of his seat until he's standing in front of me at the counter.

I ignore him, my brain struggling to wrap itself around the truth of my new reality. I'm starting to hyperventilate. I grab at my chest. My heart aches.

"Elizabeth," I whimper.

"I know, Jackie. I'm heartbroken too. I wish I could give you a big hug right now."

"It's fine." I stiffen my back and take in a long, deep breath. "I'm fine."

"Are you sure? I know how much the game means to you."

Elizabeth isn't wrong. When everything else goes sideways, Rule Them All is where everything makes sense. I've never tasted success like I have with Woman'sWorld. Some days, I think it's all I'll ever be good at. And now it's all crumbling in front of me.

"It's just a game." My voice is cold and detached. "I've got to go. I'm at work."

"Oh, okay. Call me if you need anything." I hear the concern in Elizabeth's voice and try to keep it together long enough to get her off the phone.

"Will do, Lizbit."

I hang up and pull out my email. Elizabeth was right. Right there in my email sits the notice of my world ending. *Literally.* I take a deep breath and set my phone aside with measured care.

I close my eyes and place my splayed palms on the counter.

It's gone.

"*Fuck!*" I scream at the top of my lungs.

Chapter Fifteen

Eddie

"Fuck!" Jackie howls like she's grabbed a hot poker. She throws a coffee cup against the far wall, luckily away from the few customers in the shop. Porcelain shards rain down, hitting the tile floor with a soft clink.

My heart is instantly in my throat and adrenaline has me charging toward Jackie. The urge to take care of her, keep her safe, takes over my every thought. I have completely lost whatever it was I was doing five seconds ago. All I can focus on now is Jackie, who is storming around like a wounded wild animal. She's scared and angry, lashing out at anything she can reach. All I want to do is keep her from hurting herself. Or anyone else.

"Sorry, folks, but we're going to close up for the rest of the day," I announce to the handful of customers. A couple tucked in the corner make quick work of scurrying out of the front door. I usher out the other customers with a tight smile and profuse apologies.

Once the front door is locked and the sign flipped to *Closed*, I turn my full attention to Jackie. She's broken a few more cups, but it doesn't seem to have calmed her down. Her chest is heaving like she's about to hyperventilate. Her eyes are wild and watery. I'm more scared for her than I am scared of her.

"Jackie, what's wrong?" I risk asking.

"It's gone!" she shouts to the ceiling, not acknowledging me. I shake my head, not understanding. "How could they?"

"Who?"

"This isn't right."

"What isn't?"

Jackie just howls and throws another cup. This is the worst game of twenty questions ever.

I hold up my hands and approach her slowly. She's pacing, shaking her head and tugging at her hair. She looks equal parts furious and tortured.

"What can I do to help?" I keep my voice as soft and soothing as I can. Jackie's feral gaze snaps to me, acknowledging my existence for the first time since her tantrum started.

"Slap me," she demands, taking a quick step toward me.

"What?" I jerk back, shaking my head.

"Slap me!" she shouts, charging toward me. "Right here." She taps the side of her face, hard enough to turn it a soft shade of pink.

"You're crazy. No way."

"Khakis, listen to me very carefully." She grabs a fistful of my shirt. She is close enough that I can smell her familiar coffee and caramel scent. "I'm freaking out.

My mind is going a mile a minute. I need to shut it off. I *need* you to slap me."

Her eyes hold an unnerving frenzy reflecting the panic coursing through her body. I have to do something, but I'm sure as hell not slapping her. My hands are moving before I'm aware of making a conscious decision.

I snake an arm around her waist and tug her against me. The adrenaline stinging my veins makes my movements quick and rough. My pulse pounds in every inch of my body as I slide a hand into her hair. Jackie's chest is heaving against mine. She draws in a surprised gasp, and her eyebrows knit together in confusion.

Holding her to me in a hard embrace, I seal my lips to hers, claiming the kiss I've been coveting since the first moment I met her. It's quick and aggressive like the slap she was begging me for. She lets out a startled hum, and I pull back. The shock on her face makes my heart race with fear and uncertainty. I step back, putting a few feet between us.

The coffee shop is dead quiet. The furious beating of my heart fills the room, mixed with Jackie's heavy breaths. She stares into my eyes, questioning. Challenging. Demanding. I am stripped naked by her gaze, awaiting my fate like a convicted man. A slow smile blooms across Jackie's rosy lips just before she launches herself at me.

She takes two quick steps and jumps on me, wrapping her legs around my hips and snaking her arms around my neck. I stumble back at her force. Overcompensating, I lurch forward, and we slam against the display case.

Jackie is coiled around me, pinned between my body and the curved glass. She arches her back away from the cold surface, pressing herself harder against me. The soft light of the case behind her catches the red hues in her hair and there is a devious twinkle in her eye. She looks like trouble wrapped in temptation. I crash my mouth on hers and those pillowy lips part for my eager tongue. She tastes sweet and warm and wicked, like dessert for dinner.

"Eddie." She moans my name — my actual name — grabs a handful of my hair and tugs. She's not gentle as she tightens her legs around my waist and digs her boots into my lower back. The sensation makes me desperate, and I kiss her like it's the last thing I'll ever do.

Knowing Jackie, it just might be.

"What was all that ruckus?" a man's voice calls from the back of the shop.

It snaps me out of the trance, and I pull away. Or at least I try. Jackie is too firmly glued to my body. She doesn't budge when I pull away from the display case.

Pops cocks an eyebrow and stares at the pair of us. "Pardon my interruption, but last I checked this was a reputable business establishment."

"Sir, I —" Holding my hands up in surrender, I start to explain why Jackie's wrapped around me like a boa constrictor.

"Reputable? Please," Jackie interrupts.

"Fine. A disreputable business establishment then. Which still needs to be open to conduct business," Pops retorts.

Jackie finally climbs off me and saunters over to Pops.

I fold my hands in front of me, trying like hell to hide my raging hard-on from Jackie's grandfather. I clearly fail.

"Disreputable, indeed," he purrs, staring at my crotch. Jackie traces his gaze and lets out a long, low whistle. She must've done time as a construction worker. Fully objectified, I clear my throat to bring their attention back up above my waist.

"I'm taking a mental health day," Jackie blurts out.

"I don't blame you," Pops teases.

I stand awkwardly in the middle of the coffee shop, watching this bizarre exchange like a deer in headlights. Jackie storms past Pops, stopping in front of what I assume is the back door to the shop.

"You coming, Khakis?" She crooks her finger at me with a simper before disappearing through the door.

"I'm just going to...go." I mutter as I shuffle past Pops, heading toward the doorway where Jackie disappeared.

"I don't blame you either," he says with a chuckle.

Chapter Sixteen

Jackie

I take the stairs up to my apartment two at a time, my heart racing. I know without a whisper of a doubt that Eddie will follow me. Good thing too, because otherwise I might have to murder my favorite family member for being the grandfather of all cockblockers.

That kiss. Holy hellcat!

Khakis has a few tricks up those starched dress sleeves. His tongue is a thing of beauty. And what he's packing *under* those khakis? *Yes, please.*

The way he pounced on me, like a zombie on a B-list character from *The Walking Dead*, was straight out of one of my fantasies. I guess that's what happens when I tease a strait-laced guy for days on end—he snaps in the sexiest way imaginable. The cold glass behind me, his hot body on top. *Amazing.*

The stairs creak, and I spin to see a disheveled Eddie standing in the doorway to my apartment. His shirt is untucked, his dark-brown hair sticking up in a hundred different directions. My red lipstick is smeared across his face. He looks like he's been mauled. *He kind of was.* He's downright yummy, especially with that desperate hunger in his eyes. He stalks across the room in three long strides, colliding with me at nearly full force. He slides his fingers into my hair and he kisses me again. Hard. I let out a low moan.

"You. Naked. Now," I command, shoving him away.

He takes a few steps back and, with a wide smile, starts unbuckling his pants. I stroll to my computer and queue up some mood music. Pops might know exactly what's going down up here, but he doesn't need to *hear* it too.

I'm primed and ready to get naked and horizontal when Eddie's phone rings. He pulls it out of his pocket and glances at the screen. I expect him to toss it aside. Instead, he has the audacity to answer it.

"You can't be serious," I chide. I purse my lips, and my nostrils flare as anger surges through me. He holds up a finger, telling me to wait. I imagine the snapping sound it's going to make when I break it off and shove it up his...

"Darla," Eddie says into his phone, looking down and away bashfully.

While bodily injury has its place, there is more than one way to torture a man. *Time to show Khakis what he's missing.* I kick off my loosely tied boots with a thud, drawing his eyes back to me. I flick open the button of my pants, turn around and bend forward before I slide them down, revealing my red lace panties. Eddie growls across the room. I peek over my shoulder and give him a lascivious smile. His eyes are glued to my ass.

"No, I can't," he says into the phone, his voice rough as sandpaper. "I'm not going to make it."

Spinning to face him, I tug my shirt up and over my head. Eddie's mouth drops open as he stares at the red bra that matches my panties.

"Just reschedule, damn it," he yells at whoever is on the other end of the line. With a devious smile, I unhook my bra and let it fall to the floor in front of me. Eddie's gaze is locked on the metal arrow piercings in each of my hard nipples. He lets out a low groan and adjusts his hard cock, straining against those khakis.

"Cancel everything. Indefinitely," he barks before hanging up and tossing the phone aside. It starts ringing again almost immediately, but this time he ignores it. *Smart boy.*

He crosses my small studio, eyes locked on my nipples. He cups my breasts in his warm hands, twisting each piercing and rolling it between his fingers. The sensation is absolutely amazing, but when he takes a hard nipple in his mouth and nips at it, my knees buckle. He catches me, gripping my ass with his firm hand and pulling me against him.

I fist his already wild hair and pull his face away. I run my hands down his chest, grip the sides of his shirt and rip it open. Buttons go flying in every direction. I bite my lip and look up into his dark eyes.

"I've always wanted to do that," I confess with a wide smile.

He leans down, and my bare chest brushes his. His mouth covers mine, and my lips tingle as he whispers, "I'll buy a new shirt every damn day for you to rip open if you promise to let me fuck you."

"You're naughty, aren't you, Khakis?" I tease. Our breath mingles, forming a hot, wet, storm between us.

"You have no idea."

With a sultry groan, he lifts me, wrapping my legs around his waist. He walks us to my bed before lowering me down to it with a gentle hunger. I push the rest of his shirt down off his shoulders while he fumbles with his belt. With our combined efforts, he's stripped down to his boxers in a flash. His body is firm and lean. He's not overly muscular, but he's trim in all the right places. I'm not surprised to find it void of any piercings or tattoos. Not even a tan. *Mr. Responsible.* I'm sure he always uses sunscreen.

He kisses his way down my body with furious leisure. He skates his soft lips and strong tongue across my breasts and down my stomach with delicate, torturing touches. He removes my panties with deft reverence. I spread my legs wide as he settles between them, eager for him. He bites the inside of my thigh, sucking at the sensitive skin, leaving no doubt he wants to leave a mark.

He slides his thick tongue up the length of me before circling my sensitive clit. I buck off the bed at the sensation. He holds me down with one hand, parting me with the other. The way Eddie has taken control, the confidence in his touch, is exhilarating. He devours me, lapping at my hungry wetness. He glides two fingers inside me, pumping in the same rhythm as his tongue. *This man knows what he's doing.*

I grip his short hair and grind against his mouth. I'm on the edge, close to coming, when he circles my tight hole with his thick thumb. The sensitive folds sing at the dirty caress.

"Yes," I moan, giving him permission. He thrusts into my ass in time with his fingers massaging my pussy. I feel so full. So tight. I come harder than a freight train, screaming his name at the top of my lungs. Both holes tense around his fingers.

"Eddie, yes. Fuck, yes." I'm delirious with the pleasure coursing over every inch of my body.

It takes a full five minutes to come down from my climax. He continues his slow ministrations the entire time. When I finally catch my breath, he leans back and takes in the sight of me.

"Flip over," he urges.

I obey, my brain too swamped with dopamine to argue.

He fists an ass cheek in each palm with a firm massage. I sink my chest down to the mattress and rock my hips back against him.

"Do you have a condom?"

"I'm on the pill. Are you clean?" I ask, barely caring what the answer is.

"Yes."

I twist and peer at him over my shoulder. "Fuck me raw, Eddie."

He sinks into me without a second's hesitation.

Eddie Jaworski fucks me hard and fast. He grabs my hips and drives into me with wild, animalistic strokes. The sensation is overpowering. I can't catch my breath. The second orgasm wracks my body with a surprising violence. Every muscle in my body tenses, and I swear, I speak in tongues.

We collapse in a hot mess, tangled together in satisfied exhaustion.

Chapter Seventeen

Eddie

I lie in Jackie's bed, as naked as the day I was born, wearing only a smug smile. I interlace my fingers and slip them underneath my head as a makeshift pillow. Staring up at the white ceiling, I shake my head in disbelief.

"What's with the grin, Khakis?" Jackie calls from her bathroom doorway.

Rolling to my side, I study her. She is also stark naked. And mesmerizingly beautiful. The early afternoon light filters in through the thin curtains over the window on the far side of her studio apartment. It catches the orange highlights in her hair, warms the pink glow in her cheeks and glints off her metallic nipple piercings. Just when I think she's out of surprises, this woman keeps me on my toes.

Short, curvy and pierced, she's the sexiest thing I've ever laid eyes on. Her body calls to me with a siren's song, every bit as alluring as that smart mouth and quick wit. I'm starting to think there isn't a single thing about Jackie Ryan that I don't find fascinating.

"Just happy I could be of service, Ignis," I quip.

She stalks back to the bed, crossing her legs and swaying her hips with each ruthless step.

"Desperate times call for desperate measures." Her voice is raspy and low.

"You did sound pretty desperate, what with all that panting and pleading."

She climbs on top of me, a knee on either side of my hips, and leans down over me. I steel my features despite reveling in the feel of her supple body pressed against mine. I keep my hands behind my head, grin locked in place.

"Aren't you a cocky asshole post-coital."

"I know what I'm good at. There's no shame in having pride in what you do." I wink at her, knowing it will drive her absolutely nuts.

"Let's get one thing straight, this was fun—"

"Agreed."

She narrows her eyes at me, annoyed with my interruption. "But that doesn't mean we're like…a couple or anything. We aren't *dating*." Her perfect little nose crinkles in disgust. "We're just screwing," she declares.

I roll us over and pin her to the mattress with my body. The sheets are a tangled mess underneath us. The comforter is somewhere on the floor. I don't know if she even has pillows, but they sure as hell didn't survive our workout. She wraps her legs around my waist, crossing her ankles and squeezing. She grips my shoulder with one hand and fists a tuft of my hair with the other. This woman doesn't know how to surrender.

"Just screwing?" I ask, staring down at her. I'm not surprised, but I am disappointed.

"Yes, Khakis. All sex, no feelings. Got it?"

Her voice is sweet and playful. She's taunting me. Still, there's fear hiding in those beautiful eyes. Every neuron in my brain is shouting for me to argue with her. What we are doing is so much more than sex. So much more than physical. We have a connection. And she damn well knows it. But I also know her. The harder I chase her, the faster she will run. She was born to be evasive. I'll bide my time and wait until she's too far in love with me to stop it.

I shake my head and feign shock. "But you took my virtue. I'm a tainted man now. You have to marry me, or I'll be ruined."

"You're such a dork. Shut up before you spoil it," she commands, pulling my lips down to hers.

Her words are playful, but I can't help the quiet alarm they spark in my gut. If I'm not careful, this woman really will ruin me.

Chapter Eighteen

Eddie

"How nice of you to finally show up," Darla chides.

"I'm sorry about the other day." Starting a meeting with an apology seems to be my new normal with Darla.

"Sorry for what? Canceling the publicity meeting that had been scheduled for a month with zero excuse or hanging up on me?" She leans back against her desk, arms folded and scowl in place. She's casually threatening. She has that presence that lets me know she could destroy me if she wanted to.

"Both. It was an emergency," I lie. Well, at the time it did feel like an emergency to get Jackie naked and screaming my name. The building could've been on fire, and I still wouldn't have been able to pull myself away.

"No. It wasn't." Darla levels me with a knowing glare, and I keep my mouth shut. I have no idea how she knows I was with Jackie, but I have no doubt she's figured out something is going on.

"Let's get this over with." She shoves off her desk and circles around to her chair. Lowering herself with measured control, she takes a seat. Flipping open her engraved leather portfolio, she trails a finger over her handwritten notes. "The publicist wants more personal content to post on your social media pages."

"No," I answer definitely.

"They want you to do a public appearance for publicity."

"Fuck no." Neither answer is a surprise. We've been over this a million times before. Telling the world I'm E.B. Jericho is like painting a target on my back and posting a reward for my own hide. *No thanks.*

"Do you want to be involved at all?" She slaps the portfolio shut with a surprisingly loud smack.

"As little as I can be, please. That's why I have you."

"You are infuriating, Eddie. You're expecting me to do my job with one hand tied behind my back, you realize that?"

I give her a wide smile and quip, "You're twice as good as anyone else, so it only seems fair."

"It's lucky for you that mystery sells."

"Good for both of us."

She nods in the slightest of concessions. "Have you finished the draft yet?"

"I've finished a draft." I'm intentionally evasive, but there's no point. Darla knows me too well to be fooled by a little word play.

"Goddammit, Eddie! No side projects. Not now."

"It's just something small. I can do both." *I think.*

"You better." Darla shakes her head and sighs. "Now get out of my office."

"Yes, Boss."

Feeling like a fresh parolee, I make a dash for the door before she can change her mind.

* * * *

Jackie is dancing around the coffee shop, singing along with the 1990s music she always has playing when she's working. I've managed to get zero work done today, too busy watching her. I'm close to missing a deadline for the first time in my life and I don't care. I'm having too much fun chasing Jackie Ryan.

Every time she dances close, I reach out and try to catch her. Each time she slips away, wiggling her finger at me with a tsk.

"Nah-ah. Get back to work, Khakis. That capital won't venture itself," she chides. Hopping up to sit on the counter, she smiles at me.

I make a loud buzzing noise. "Wrong again, Ignis."

This is my favorite time of day, late morning. After the morning rush — I use the term loosely — and before Jesús shows up. The two of us are alone in the cafe, teasing and taunting each other.

I cross the shop to her. With a hand on either side of her thighs, I cage her in and lean down for a kiss. She pulls away, keeping things on her terms.

With a head-tilt and a side-eye she tells me, "I'm starting to think you're secretly a superhero."

I glance around quickly before holding my index finger up to my lips and shushing her with a lopsided grin. I've been called worse.

Jackie tugs on the lapel of my button-down. "I'm on to you and your mild-mannered alter ego." She brings her lips to mine, and whispers, "Captain Khakis.

Defender of the pocket protector. Savior of the pleated pant."

"Destroyer of Ignis' panties."

She laughs, pushes me away and hops off the counter. "In your dreams, Khakis."

"Among other places," I tease.

She giggles as she struts away. I watch the sway of her hips with admiration. I shake my head and try to focus on anything other than wanting to carry her upstairs and bury myself deep inside her for the rest of my life.

"So, what's the deal with all this junk?" I ask to change the subject. I gesture to the chaotic wall of memorabilia behind us.

"Junk!" She gasps. "Excuse you. Those are collectors' items, thank you very much."

"Oh really?" I point to the faded subway ticket from the 1980s.

"Each item on that wall has a story," she explains. She storms over, her boot-clad feet pounding on the old wood floor. Stepping in next to me, she cocks a hip out and jabs a finger into the wall. "That was the first time Pops rode the New York subway. Ask him about it, he's always looking for new victims to torture with his stories."

"An experience worth immortalizing, no doubt." I lean against the wall and cross my arms.

"Not everything in life is sugar and spice. Good things can be dark and gritty too." She too leans against the wall, crossing her arms and mocking me.

"You don't say." I hook a finger in one of her belt loops and pull her closer to me. She keeps her arms folded, preventing me from feeling her body pressed against mine like I'd hoped. "Tell me more, wise one."

She shakes her head. Reaching up on her tiptoes, she wraps her arms around my neck and tugs on the ends of my hair. "Expand your horizons. Try something new. Get a tattoo. Go to a concert. Eat street food. Live dangerously. Wear white after Labor Day." She fake-gasps and slaps a hand over her mouth.

"You sound like Ben. He's got this idiotic idea that you're only living if you're torturing yourself with new experiences." I rub my nose against hers, encouraging her to tilt her head back for a kiss.

"Sounds like Ben might be my type." With her lips grazing mine, she asks, "Can I have his number?"

"Sure, let me see." I reach into my pocket. When I pull out my hand, I'm holding up my middle finger right in front of her face. With a sweet smile, I add, "Here you go."

She bites her lip to stifle a chuckle. She grabs my hand and shoves it back down to my side. When she lets go, I intertwine our fingers. I hold her hand, rubbing small circles with my thumb. We're both staring down at the soft caress. There's an intimacy in the innocent touch, a comfort to the feel of her hand in mine.

"Fine. JC called dibs anyway. But I'm with Ben. A little bit of recklessness would do you good, Khakis."

"You've got it all figured out, don't you? You know how everyone else should live their life."

"Yep. Sure do," she answers, her voice soft and low.

"Well, excuse me if I don't take advice from the woman who can't find a matching pair of socks to save her life."

"Tiny details. I don't sweat the small stuff." She draws me to her, my irresistible temptation.

"Whatever you say, Buddha. By the way, your shirt's on inside out."

"Laundry day," is her explanation.

I'm laughing when I finally kiss her, those full lips torturing me with their taste as much as their words.

Chapter Nineteen

Jackie

"I've got a bet for you," I call out to Eddie as soon as he walks in the door to the coffee shop. I've decided to use and abuse him. I need to focus on anything other than how pissed I am that some corporate asshat is cancelling my game. I've always found orgasms are the best distraction.

"Good morning to you too." He sets his bag down at his usual table. I stalk up to him, wrap a leg around his hip and pull him into a deep kiss—porno tongue included.

"I want you to guess how many piercings I have. And, if I win, you come to a concert with me. Ben was right, you need to expand your horizons. And I have magnanimously decided I'm just the girl to do it." Really, I just can't be alone in my apartment for a second or I'll go completely insane.

"I like my horizons right where they are, thank you very much." He grabs my ass and buries his face in the crook of my neck. He takes a deep breath and nips at the sensitive skin. I moan at the soft tickle.

"Oh, come on, Khakis. Where is your sense of adventure?"

"Hiding under the couch at home, terrified of you. Where's your rationality?"

I groan. "It ran away to join the circus. Why do you have to be so boring?" I ask, hopping off him and turning to walk away. He snakes an arm around my waist and pulls me against him, nuzzling back into my neck.

"Fine. What do I get if I win?" he asks with exhausted reservation.

"What do you want?" I wiggle my hips against him, hoping it will be something deliciously naughty. The heavy pause while he thinks of his prize makes me nervous.

"If I win, we go to Sunday brunch."

I scoff. "Whatever. Total weak-sauce, Khakis. I love pancakes."

"Then we have a deal."

That was easier than I thought it would be. Eddie has no idea what he's getting himself into agreeing to go to a concert with me. Everyone should experience a mosh pit at least once in their life.

"Okay, smarty pants. What's your guess?" I've got this one in the bag. Eddie knows about a few of my piercings. He's quite a fan of the bars through my nipples. But I've got a helix piercing in my ear that I don't usually keep any jewelry in. I'm sure he has no idea.

"Hmmm…" He pushes me away, hands on my hips. He spins me in a slow circle, examining every inch of my body before turning me to face him. "Let me think."

"Any day, Khakis." I tap my foot.

"Eight," he declares. My jaw drops to the floor.

"How did you know that?"

"Two in each ear. The nose ring is obvious." He grins, leaning in and whispering in my ear, "And I'm very familiar with your nipple piercings."

"That's only seven. You can't count."

He shrugs. "I added one for good measure since you seemed too cocky for your own good."

I shove him away. "You're such a pain in the ass!"

His warm laugh makes my skin heat. I turn and storm off.

"I'll pick you up at nine-thirty."

* * * *

Eddie opens the door for me like the dork that he is, and I step into "the club". That's where he decided to take me for our brunch bet, a country club. I knew Khakis wasn't going to let me get away with a Denny's pancake special, but a stuffy country club? So not my scene. The blue hairs seem to agree. My all-black attire isn't making me any friends.

"Think a few cloth napkins and dainty teacups are going to intimidate me, Khakis? You wish," I croon into his ear as we follow the hostess to our table.

"Not at all, Ignis. I just think you should expand your horizons." He pulls out the chair for me, and I take a seat. He leans over and tucks a strand of hair behind my ear before adding, "And I have magnanimously decided I'm just the guy to do it."

"Hardy-har-har, Smart ass."

He smirks behind his menu. "Plus, this place has the best Belgian waffles in the world."

"I'm regretting this outing slightly less now." I'm pretty far outside my comfort zone here, but I take it in stride. The opinion of strangers has never mattered much to me anyway.

Our server doesn't get a full sentence out before I'm handing her our menus.

"Round of Belgian waffles for the table, and don't skimp on the whipped cream, my friend."

The twenty-something looks me up and down, probably wondering if she should call security, before turning to Eddie for the adult decision. It's infuriating.

"You heard the lady," Eddie tells her with a smile. I like him more than I did five minutes ago. And more than I did the day before that, and the week before that. Khakis seems to be growing on me at an alarming rate. *Nah. That's just the orgasms talking. Fight your biology, woman!*

"Are you one of those trust fund kids?" I squeeze my lemon wedge into my ice water, swirl it and take a long drag.

"How's that now?" Eddie drapes his napkin in his lap like a good boy and proceeds to butter us each a scone.

"You know, one of those stupid rich guys whose great-great-grandfather invented the zipper or something and now the rest of you are completely worthless, aimlessly wandering through life with no sense of purpose."

"Oh, one of those." He nods a few times teasing me, before shaking his head and laughing. "Where do you get this stuff?"

"The mind of a creative genius is a wondrous thing."

"You don't say. And no, I didn't grow up rich."

I narrow my eyes at him, waiting for the *but* I feel he owes me. Instead, he hands me my buttered scone and doesn't say any more. Annoyed, I tear the scone in half with a grunt.

"You know, it doesn't matter if you are. I only like you for one thing anyway."

"My wit?" he asks.

"Your cock," I correct.

Eddie chokes on the sip of coffee he'd just taken. He should've known better than to drink before I'd delivered my punchline.

"Besides, my best friend Elizabeth is stupid rich, and she hasn't let it turn her into a prissy bitch. It doesn't have to ruin you."

"You think money ruins people?" Eddie asks me, his voice and features more serious than I am ready for on a Sunday morning.

"I think it amplifies whatever you are without it. Elizabeth is generous with her heart and her money. Her dad is a festering bag of shit."

"You've got great table conversation. I'm so glad we get to share a meal together."

I shrug and take the first bite of my buttery scone.

"Holy blessed mother of baked goods, that's amazing!" The light, fluffy morsel is still warm and practically melts in my mouth. A mixture of sweet and salty, it is the perfect combination. My mouth waters, and I let out a not-so-subtle moan of ecstasy.

Eddie leans back and eats his scone while managing to keep a smug grin on his face. It'd be annoying if I weren't in pastry heaven.

If the scones were heaven, the waffles are the devil's playground. A rich, creamy, decadent guilty pleasure that brought this woman to gastronomic nirvana. The outsides are a crispy golden brown, but the inside is a dense, moist cake. Miniature chocolate chips, pure maple syrup and thick whipped cream fill every delicious square. I make inappropriate noises throughout the entirety of brunch. People scurry by our table like I'm doing a naked back-handspring. *Fuck 'em. These are the best waffles of my life!*

"They're quite good, aren't they?" a little old lady who could be a lookalike for Betty White asks from beside Eddie.

I have manners enough to swallow down my last bite before answering, "Positively sinful."

"Grandma!" Eddie stands up and gives her a warm hug.

"Grandma?" I choke on my lemon water. I cough the water out of my lungs, and it dribbles down my chin. The room is suddenly a thousand degrees. Posh strangers are one thing. Eddie's sweet old grandmother is another.

"Hello, Eddie, darling. Sasha said you were here with a young woman, and I couldn't resist sneaking a peek. Is this your girlfriend?"

"She's —" Eddie doesn't get a chance to answer.

"Fuck no," I blurt out. I hate being called somebody's anything. I'm me. Jackie Ryan. Not my mother's daughter. Not Eddie's girlfriend. I don't need someone else's expectations running how I live my life.

"Gee, thanks," he scoffs, more hurt than insulted, I think, slumping back down in his chair.

His grandma flicks her gaze back and forth between the two of us for a long moment before she finally cracks up laughing. Whether it's at me or Eddie, I'm not sure.

"She's plucky. I like her." She wags a wrinkled finger in my face. "Bring her next month to your mother's little party. She'll make it a bit more lively."

"Grandma, that's not exactly Jackie's scene."

"What's not?" I chime in, frustrated I'm the subject of the conversation going on right in front of me.

"My mother is hosting a dinner party." Eddie crosses his arms and leans across the table. A challenge.

"And what makes you think I wouldn't enjoy your mother's dinner party?"

Eddie doesn't answer. He just cocks an eyebrow and stares at me with that *seriously?* expression of his. How a man can be so aggravating without even saying a word is beyond me. It must be Captain Khakis' superpower.

"Jackie…it is Jackie, right?" his grandma asks.

"That's me. Jackie Ryan, at your service."

"Evelyn Zielinski. A pleasure to meet you." She holds out her hand, and I shake it, giving her a smile. I kind of like this quirky old woman. "Jackie, trust me, no one enjoys Edith's dinner parties except Edith. But it would make the evening of an old lady much more entertaining if you would oblige us with your company. I promise to keep you well fed with all the pigs in blankets you could want and well plied with wine."

"With an offer like that, how could I possibly say no?"

"Fabulous. We'll see you next month."

"Nice to meet you, Evelyn."

"Same to you, Jackie."

Before leaving, Evelyn leans down and whispers something in Eddie's ear. I twist in my seat, a sick feeling twirling around the waffles in my stomach knowing I'm the subject of their tête-à-tête.

"I know," he answers with that boyish grin of his.

"Good boy," she coos before patting him on the shoulder and disappearing. I don't give him the satisfaction of asking what she said, although I admit I'm rather desperate to know.

"Explain to me again how you're *not* a trust fund kid when your grandma seems to be a regular here?" I try to put him on the defensive.

"I never said I didn't have money." He sits down, delicately laying his napkin back in his lap. I wait for him to go on, but when he doesn't, I prod again.

"So, you shit gold nuggets or something, Khakis?"

He lets out an awkward chuckle. "Not that I'm aware of."

I keep him pinned with my gaze, refusing to let it go until he gives me some sort of answer.

"The truth is I grew up kind of poor. My mom got pregnant young, and my dad ghosted. So we lived with my grandparents. When I made a little money, I wanted to spoil my family. So, I buy my grandma a membership to this club every year as a Christmas gift."

I'm not going to lie, the tenderness in his voice and the openness of his words make me go all soft and mushy inside.

"They serve breakfast all day and she likes hustling the other grannies at shuffleboard. Don't ever play her for money," he adds under his breath with that boyish grin that sets my panties on fire.

There is something about Eddie's honest vulnerability that makes me want to know more. For us to *be* more. I kick away the errant fantasy like it's a shark out for blood. Khakis is a distraction. Nothing more.

Chapter Twenty

Eddie

"You can get naked or you can get out. The choice is yours. You've got to the count of ten," Jackie crows at me. She's standing in the middle of her bed wearing nothing but her bra and panties and a pair of long red satin gloves. They match her fiery hair and her scarlet lips.

"Haven't you heard you catch more flies with honey than with vinegar?" I tsk while unbuttoning my shirt. I'm a smartass, but I'm not stupid. If Jackie tells me to get naked, I oblige. We've been playing this game of hers for a few weeks now. Sex on her terms — meaning no feelings. No emotions. She thinks it's working, that she can keep her distance. I hope she's wrong.

"That is a bullshit old-wives' tale. Balsamic vinegar will catch more flies, so suck it. Besides, haven't you heard you get more with a kind word and a gun than a kind word alone?"

"Says who?"

"Al Capone."

"Personal hero?"

"Occasional inspiration." She makes finger guns and mimics taking aim and blowing me away. I grab my heart and stumble back with a groan.

She giggles and holsters her imaginary weapons. She hops off the bed and stalks up to me. The sexy strut she does kills me and she knows it. I drink in every inch of her curvy body. She slides her hands up my bare chest, over my shoulders and pushes my open shirt off to the floor.

"You're such a dork." Her soft words are a warm whisper against my lips.

I grip her ass with both hands and haul her against me. I nip at her full bottom lip and tell her with a dry rasp, "You know you love it."

"I tolerate it. A good fuck buddy is hard to find," she deadpans.

I growl and back her into the bed. Three large steps, and she trips onto the mattress. Lying there, propped up on her elbows, one knee bent and legs slightly parted, she's a temptress. My naughty dream come to life.

"If I'm such a bother..." I trail my fingers along the inside of her thigh until I hit the soft fabric of her panties. "I could just leave you to your own devices."

Jackie drops her head back and lets out a soft moan when I give her core a firm stroke. I pull away and stand over her, waiting for her to admit how much she wants it. Ignis isn't one for confessing weakness. Instead, she reaches forward, grabs the waistband of my pants and pulls me down on top of her. She wraps her legs around my hips and rocks into me.

"Less talky. More fucky."

"You make me feel so tawdry," I half-tease. I know she's using me to avoid thinking about her game, her drawing, her job, her life. All those things that are too big and too scary, so she pretends they don't exist. I have to chip away that the armor she has built up against the world. "You know, a lot of people enjoy my conversational skills."

She shuts me up with a hard kiss, her sweet mouth battling with mine. Everything about this woman is a fight.

"I have other plans for your tongue."

She unhooks her ankles from around my waist and lets her legs fall open. Not missing the less-than-subtle invitation, I kiss my way down her body. When I reach the end of the bed, I slide onto my knees.

Nestled between her thighs, I peer up her beautiful body. Those deep eyes are watching me. She likes watching. Keeping eye contact, I drag my tongue up the length of her panties, tasting her wetness already. She fists my hair and tugs hard when I pull the fabric away from her soft skin. I slide a finger into her warmth and lap at her slick folds. She bites down on her bottom lip and lets out a low groan. I love her responses. Feeling her body tighten, listening to her noises, I navigate her body like a seasoned traveler, guiding her to pleasure. She comes undone for me within minutes.

The sound of her eager moans and heavy breaths gets me hard, but I can't give in. If we have sex, the night is done and I'm not ready for this game to be over. I crawl up the bed next to her. She lies back and closes her eyes. Her guard is down, and I seize the opportunity.

"Which one was your first?" I ask, tracing the outline of the tattoo on her hip.

A soft smile curls the edge of her beautiful mouth. With her eyes still closed, her fingers find the delicate flag etched on her left rib cage. It is a knife and a tube of lipstick crossed on a field of orange with two horizontal yellow stripes. The drips of blood falling off the blade match the lipstick exactly.

"What is it?" I ask, keeping my voice even and uninterested to avoid revealing how much I care. Not just about her tattoos, but her history. Her life.

"The flag for Woman'sWorld. My country in Rule Them All..." She trails off, her voice carrying the twinge of sorrow. I'm starting to understand that the game is a huge part of her life. I wonder if that's where she first tried on this badass, too-cool-to-care persona she uses to keep everyone at arm's length.

Trying to sidestep the conversational landmine of a topic, I kiss the black letters on the inside of her wrist. *Still, I rise.* "What about this one?"

"Hmm," she hums as my lips tickle her skin. She looks down at the tattoo like she forgot it was there. "That one has two meanings. First, because it's an awesome poem and a kick-ass message."

"And second?" I ask, eager to know anything—everything—about this crazy woman.

A wry smile teases her lips. "In case of a zombie apocalypse. Can't say I didn't warn 'em."

I let out a loud chuckle. I'm falling hard for this woman.

Chapter Twenty-One

Jackie

I come back from the bathroom after freshening up and Eddie is sprawled out on my bed in his boxers, my well-worn copy of *Syrion's Raider* in his hands. It's E.B. Jericho's first book in the *Sins of Tomorrow* series and my all-time favorite. I have several copies, but the hardbound one in his hands is my most treasured. I've read it dozens of times. It has a perpetual place of honor on my nightstand. Any time I can't sleep, I pick it up and turn to a random page. The familiar words are more comforting than a warm blanket or a soft lullaby.

Part of me wants to snap at him to put down the treasure, but he handles it with a gentle care so instead I lean against the door jamb, cross my arms, and watch him. He has one leg under the tangled mess of sheets, meaning a crumpled map of Woman'sWorld trails up his body. The custom sheets were a Christmas gift from Elizabeth, and I make a mental note to tell her that

Herlandia, my capital city, just happened to land on Eddie's junk. *The convergence of two of my favorite places.*

His other leg is bent at the knee with his boxers riding up his muscular thigh. He has my extra pillow folded up and tucked under his head. He's a big guy, but he's not a bed hog. He's left enough room for me to slide back in next to him.

There is something endearing about the way he's made himself at home in my space. We always meet up at my place. If we were dating, I'd be wondering why he never asks me to his place. I'd be getting some major Norman Bates vibes. But we're just fucking. When I want. Where I want. I've made him come to me, on my terms. Yet he manages to acquiesce with an aggravating air of victory, as if every booty call is his only little triumph.

If I were smart, I'd kick him out right now. He's provided the toe-curling distractions I keep him around for. He has no other reason to loiter in my bed. Unfortunately, I'm less and less eager to kick him out with each orgasm. And there have been *a lot*. He reads my body as easily as he's reading my favorite book.

My lady parts hum with contentment at the recent memory. And much to my horror, my heart flutters in my chest. Luckily my head is still functioning, and I lock that shit down.

"Make yourself right at home," I tease him.

"Will do, thanks," he calls back without bothering to look up from his book. I don't miss the way the side of his mouth tips up in a smirk. *Smartass.*

I climb onto the bed and scoot up next to him.

"Don't you have a life you need to get back to?" I ask, poking him in the ribs.

"Nope. I'm good." He turns the page and keeps reading.

I bite back a smile. When was it that I started wanting him to stay? I've made a point of shoving him out the door as soon as his dick goes soft. Who needs to cuddle? Somewhere along the way I've gotten used to having him here. Somehow, I've started to like having him in my bed, even after the sex. It's possible I might actually like spending time with the human equivalent of vanilla pudding. The idea is a little unsettling.

"I haven't read this one in awhile." Eddie's voice pulls me out of my thoughts. "I like reading your copy, with all your little notes and underlines. It almost feels like reading your diary. *Persei held her cold blade steady against the warlord's throat, smiling when his flinch caused the steel to break the pale skin. Watching his orange blood ooze out of the fresh wound, she knew it was going to be a good day.* You even put a little heart next to that one."

"He had it coming." I shrug. "It's my favorite."

"In the series?"

"In any series. It's my favorite book."

"Wow." Eddie's arms go limp, and the book falls to his lap.

"You can't be surprised." I gesture to my walls and the dozens of half-finished drawings that cover them, most of them of Persei.

"I knew you were a fan. I just didn't realize..." He looks around the room at all my sketches like he just realized they were there. He has a goofy smile on his face, not the amused one he has when he comes up with a clever retort. This one is innocent and sweet, like when you tell a five-year-old you like their unrecognizable drawing of an elephant. He gets up and wanders around the room, taking a long look at each drawing. It makes my skin itch for reasons I can't explain. I don't give a fuck what Khakis thinks of my art.

"These are amazing. I can't believe you've never won the cover competition."

"Probably has something to do with never entering." I flop back on my bed with a quick exhale and stare up at the ceiling.

"What?" Eddie shrieks. "What do you mean?"

"What do *you* mean, what do I mean?"

"Jackie—" I know that exasperated tone. Eventually everyone who's around me long enough uses it. The frustrated, disappointed tone. The *why do you have to make everything so difficult* tone.

"Don't you dare." I jump off the bed and charge over to him.

"I didn't—"

"Oh yes, you did." I shove him back against the wall and step into his bare chest. "You don't get to judge me from up in your elitist tower. You don't know how hard it is to pour your heart and soul into something then send it out in the world to be judged, torn down and destroyed."

"I—" His voice is softer now, with a twinge of remorse. "I'm sorry."

I step back, caught off guard by his apology. We stare at each other for a moment, surrounded in a rare awkward silence. The sun has set, and the room is lit only by the dim light from my bathroom. His face is a soft shadow, and I study its curves with a sudden fascination. I have the urge to be with him. Not to fuck. This time, I want him to make love to me. *Nope.*

"Damn right you are." I spin away and storm off. Well, as far away as I can get in my tiny studio apartment.

I rip a picture off the wall and stare at it in the darkness. I can't remember what I hated about this one. At first, it looks perfect. But I keep looking and realize the perspective is off. And the shading is weak. It's not good enough. I tear it in half over and over until it is nothing but tiny shreds in my palms.

"Hey, don't do that!" Eddie is behind me in a flash, wrapping his hands around my wrists to still my self-destruction.

"Why not? It was crap," I growl.

"It was beautiful."

He tightens his grip, pulling me against his warm chest, and kisses my bare shoulder.

"It's not good enough. None of these are good enough." *I'm not good enough.*

"Says who?"

I don't have an answer. I've never shown my sketches to anyone that matters. I only painted the mural downstairs because Pops begged me, and JC dared me.

"Says me." I lift my chin and grit my teeth. My own hardest critique. "This is the last book in the *Sins of Tomorrow* series. The finale. The cover has to be perfect."

"It's just a book."

"Urgh, you just don't get it." I try to pull away, but he won't let me.

"I get that it is important to you. But I'm telling you, you're capable of so much more."

Hearing him say those words means more than I would've realized. More than I'm willing to admit. I can feel it, the wall inside me crumbing. My self-reliance failing. My resistance slipping.

He holds me in the dim room, the heavy silence falling on us like a protective cloak. My mind fills with past failures and risks not taken, the memories drowning me in a tide of regret. I will myself not to drown, not to be washed away in the flood of sadness.

"I'm tired," I whisper, sinking back into him. I don't mean I'm sleepy. I mean I'm tired of trying so hard. Of being so scared. Of giving up so easily. Of hating myself for it.

"Let's go to bed."

Eddie guides me back to the bed. A calmness washes over me when he climbs in beside me and wraps me in his comforting arms. His steady snoring is my lullaby. In the morning, before I'm fully awake, I reach out for him. The relief in my heavy heart when he is still holding me could fill the known universe three times over.

Eddie Jaworski came into my life as a passing amusement. Then I used him as a much-needed distraction. Now he has dug his way into my heart and set up camp. I don't know how to chase him out. What's worse, I don't know if I even want to.

Chapter Twenty-Two

Eddie

I'm trying to work, my laptop propped up on my legs while I'm reclining in Jackie's bed, but I can't help stealing glances at her. She's playing Rule Them All and watching her is enthralling. I feel like Dorothy peeking behind the curtain and realizing the wizard is just a man. I get why the game is a big part of her life. It's the only place she seems to truly trust herself, to take risks. I see why she's going to miss it so much.

"I can feel you watching me, creeper," Jackie taunts me without turning around.

"Just trying to capture all the new swear words and epithets. I'm petitioning Webster's to start a salty gamer edition."

"Fuck off, you human equivalent of elevator music."

"You wound me." I place the back of my hand against my forehead and pretend to wilt. "I'm writing that one down." I shift my eyes to my screen and pretend to type.

Jackie saunters over and closes my laptop, nearly taking my fingertips off in the process.

"Bullshit. We both know you can't get enough of me." She pouts her red lips and leans in. I tuck a strand of hair behind her ear and kiss her, soft and sweet. She lets out a gentle moan.

"I can't help it. You're just such a sweetheart." I kiss the tip of her nose. "And cute as a button."

"Don't make me drag the coffee grinder up here."

I chuckle out loud and she gives me that devious smile that undoes me.

"Come on, I need caffeine."

She grabs my hand and drags me down the stairs to the shop. Jackie slips behind the counter and gets to work on her cappuccino and my black coffee.

Jesús is working alone this morning and gives me two thumbs-up. I return the greeting with a wave and a big grin. It's good to know he's rooting for me. I can use all the help I can get.

Jackie holds out my coffee but pulls it away before I can grab it.

"Not so fast. No free rides. You've gotta earn it, Khakis."

She leans across the counter and runs her wet pink tongue across her top lip, leaving it glistening and tempting.

I match her pose, leaning into her across the counter.

"Is that so?" My voice is a low, sultry rumble. I slide my fingers into her hair, pull her mouth to mine and take it in a rough, demanding kiss. I claim Jackie and love every second of it.

"Incoming," JC calls out to us, covered by the world's worst fake cough.

Jackie pulls away to catch sight of an older woman in a tailored jacket, sensible loafers and nicely creased slacks.

"Fuck me gently with a chainsaw," Jackie groans, her whole body stiffening. Before I can even ask who it is, she ducks and disappears behind the counter.

"Jacqueline Marie Ryan, you can't hide from your mother."

That's Jackie's mom? She's Jackie's complete opposite. Strait-laced and put-together. I bet *she* has an IRA.

"Not hiding, just dropped a contact," Jackie retorts without standing up.

"You don't wear glasses," I tell her, earning me a *colorful* reply that would make sailors blush.

The older lady turns her attention to me.

"Marjorie Ryan, Jacqueline's mother." She holds out her hand, giving me a genial smile.

"Edwin Jaworski." I shake her hand and return the friendly greeting.

"*Edwin?*" Jackie asks, popping up like a sprung jack in the box. She looks at me confused, as if the name doesn't fit. I agree. I was named after Buzz Aldrin the astronaut, my grandfather's idea. I loved the man, but there's a reason I go by Eddie.

"Boyfriend?" Marjorie asks, her smile morphing into a sly grin.

I open my mouth to answer, but don't get the chance.

"Fuck buddy," Jackie blurts out.

I recoil from her words. It's a sharp slap across the face. *Still with this bullshit?* After weeks of spending nearly every minute together, I thought we were more. I thought we were falling for each other. But apparently we are right back to square one. *Damn.* That hurts.

"What?" she asks, somehow surprised at the betrayal written across my face.

"Just having a nasty déjà vu. I feel like we've been over this already."

"You'll have to excuse my daughter. I swear, I didn't raise her to be this inconsiderate."

"Hi, Mom. Always such a joy to see you. What can I do for you this morning?" Jackie asks, her voice coated in sarcasm.

"Just here to make sure my only child is still alive, seeing as how she refuses to take my phone calls." Marjorie's words are a sugar-coated ghost pepper. They sound sweet, but they will burn a person up from the inside.

"I've been busy."

"You must be swamped with lucrative graphic design offers, seeing as how you didn't bother to call the contact I gave you who was paying nicely for some freelance work. And apparently, it isn't a new *relationship* keeping you unavailable."

"We're—" Suddenly defensive, I start in, but don't make it very far.

"Don't," Jackie warns. "Well, Mom, I'm alive. Guilt trip received. So sorry I dodged your calls and missed out on hearing the pep talk earlier. Now if you'll excuse me, I'm going to have kinky pre-marital sex with someone I'm *not* in a relationship with."

Jackie abandons her cappuccino—and me—and disappears up the stairs at the back of the shop. I'm dumbstruck.

"Mrs. Ryan, it was a pleasure?" It comes out as an unintentional question. It is interesting to see another piece of Jackie's life revealed, but I'm also frustrated with her and for her. On one hand, her mom is a piece of work. On the other, she still won't even admit we are in a relationship.

I turn to follow Jackie up the stairs when Marjorie reaches out to stop me. She clutches my arm in a firm grip despite her manicured nails.

"Eddie, I'm…" She takes a deep breath and stares up at the ceiling. "I'm sorry. My daughter and I don't communicate very well, as you can see."

"Clearly."

"She's always been headstrong."

"Wonder where she could get that from?" I quip.

"Touché." She folds her hands in front of her, and I catch the same amused smile Jackie always tries to hide when I say something clever. "Could you just tell me one thing? Is she doing well? Is she happy?"

I glance back at the empty doorway Jackie made her escape through a few moments ago.

"Most days, yeah. I hope so, anyway."

"Thank you." She lets out a pained breath and gives me a sad smile before leaving.

The door to Jackie's apartment is ajar. Inside she's pacing the small space like a caged tiger. I shut the door with a loud thud to catch her attention.

"What took you so long?" Jackie starts in with an accusing tone.

"Sorry, Master," I bite out, pulling my shoulders back and lowering my voice. I'm in no mood to humor my *fuck buddy*. "I was trying not to be a gaping asshole to *your* mother."

"Please tell me you didn't tell her anything."

"She asked if you were happy. I said I thought so."

She tugs at her hair and groans. "Why would you say that?"

"Because it's true," I tell her flatly. "You can keep pretending this doesn't mean anything to you, but I know you're happy. With me."

"Not very happy with you right now." She crosses her arms and glares at me.

"Pissed off is your default setting. You know what I mean. With us."

"Whatever, fine, you're my boyfriend and you make me happy — most of the time. That's not the point! She doesn't need to know that."

"Wait, what? Now I'm your boyfriend?"

"Sure, the meaningless, antiquated label is all yours." She rolls her eyes at me trying to make light of the title she's been avoiding for weeks. "You practically live here these days anyway."

"But you just called me your fuck buddy."

"To my mom, yeah."

"Why? She's your mom."

"Exactly."

"I'm so confused." My head is spinning. I've got emotional whiplash. "So, just to recap, I'm your boyfriend. I make you happy. But you don't want your mother to know any of that?"

"Now he gets it!"

"Because…" I wave my hand in a go-on motion.

"Because you're too fucking perfect."

I nod a couple of times, then squeeze my eyes shut and shake my head until my neck hurts. I feel like I've got a wicked brain freeze trying to understand this crazy woman.

"You're exactly the kind of guy she wants me to be with," Jackie tells me in complete annoyance and frustration. I'm perfect, and she's pissed about it.

"And that's a problem because?"

"Because now she'll double down on her nagging for me to *grow up* and be perfect. I bet she's out there plotting our fairytale wedding, shopping for the colonial-style house we'll buy and naming the two-point-five grandkids we'll give her! And when this turns to shit and none of that happens, it will be all *my* fault. It will be because I screwed up. *Again.*"

"You know, you're a lot like a candy bar — half sweet and half nuts. What makes you think this will turn to shit?"

"Because relationships *always* do."

"Then what the hell are we even doing?" I ask, not entirely sure I want to know her answer.

"Honestly, I have no goddamn idea."

My heart breaks with her admission and all I can do is walk away.

Chapter Twenty-Three

Jackie

Eddie took off a few hours ago and all I have the energy for is staring up at the ceiling and listening to angry chick rock. I'm too anxious to sit still and too listless to be productive so I'm just wallowing in a constant state of frump. I call up Elizabeth for a video chat because what are friends for if not to share suffering with?

"Hey, Jackie. Everything okay?" my best friend asks. I rarely call her — most of our chats happen through the game. We haven't talked much since Rule Them All announced it was ending in a few months. I should be playing as much as possible, clinging to the last few minutes of my favorite pastime. Instead, I'm cutting myself off cold turkey. I'll log in and conquer a few countries when the craving gets out of control, but otherwise I'm MIA. Why bother putting energy into something I know is going to end? Ghosting the game means I've been inadvertently avoiding Elizabeth too.

"My life is a rose-colored pile of shit," I brood.

"Is that better or worse than regular poo?"

I smile at her inability to swear even a little. She's the good one, the angel on my shoulder.

"Worse, my angel. So much worse. You know what you're getting with a regular lumpy, corn-filled load. But when it's rose-colored, you can almost convince yourself it's not that bad. Then, you get a big smelly whiff and gag on the reality of it."

"I get it. I'm sad too. I kept hoping we could crowd-source the funding to keep Rule Them All going. It just doesn't look possible. We'd have to raise like a hundred million dollars."

I'd almost forgotten that the game was getting shutdown. Eddie is an even better distraction when he's pissed at me than when he's inside me. *Go figure.* That's all I really wanted with him, a distraction, but now he's almost more of a catastrophe than losing my game. I let out a long sigh and brace myself for the humiliation that will ensure after confessing to Elizabeth that I'm having boy trouble.

"Is it something else?" my very intuitive friend asks.

"No, just going to miss destroying all the dipshits of the gaming world with my feminine superiority." I chicken out. She's in love with her ideal guy, literally. She has the spreadsheets to prove it. She's going to be no help in the commiseration of how inferior men are as a gender.

"For what it's worth, you'll always be my favorite dictatoress." She gives me one of her wide, genuine smiles. Despite the toilet my life currently seems to be circling, she makes me feel a little bit better.

"Thanks, Lizbit."

A knock on my front door makes my heart stutter. Across the inside of my brain, my masochistic subconscious plasters the image of Eddie standing on the other side of the door.

"I gotta run. I'll catch you later."

I spring off the bed and charge to my door, throwing it open with a wry smile. It fades to a disappointed frown at the sight of Pops standing in the hallway.

"Oh, hi," I mumble before skulking across the room.

"Were you expecting the queen?" Pops call after me.

"A Nigerian prince actually." I pinch my eyebrows together and scratch my chin. "His email said he'd pay me back double what I loaned him as soon as he made it to America."

"I wouldn't hold your breath," Pops teases. "I heard you got a visit from your mom today."

I nod. He takes a seat on the bed and pats the spot next to it. "And how did that go?"

"She met Khakis." I flop down on the bed, grab my pillow and scream into it.

"And why is that so bad?" His voice is gentle and cajoling despite knowing exactly how I feel about my mother and her expectations for my life.

I toss the pillow aside and stare up at the ceiling. "Because I don't need one more thing she can hang over my head for screwing up. You know how she is."

"Don't count your failures before they hatch, kiddo. And even if things don't work out with Eddie, there's no shame in chasing love."

"Love's not my bag. That's the point. I'm just having fun."

"What's wrong with love?" Pops admonishes. He pokes me in the ribs with that damn cane, and I groan.

I sit up and answer with my canned response. "Love is for suckers. It's a manufactured construct to secure the patriarchal infrastructure and convince us monogamy is sustainable and marriage is anything other than a prison."

Pops tsks. "How did someone so young get so jaded?"

"I speak as I find. Robert is a lying dickweed coward who left Mom's life a disaster. And bullshit society expectations kept you from finding your soulmate." I sink back down into the bed and throw my arms over my face in a pointless attempt to keep away the memories. I haven't thought about my dad in a long time, but his betrayal still stings. Cheating is a major douche canoe move, but I can at least understand the allure of carnal sin. What I don't get is leaving your only daughter without so much as a *seeya later, kid.*

"I will grant you that your father is a monumental piece of shit. But I'll have you know I had twenty-six wonderful years with my soulmate."

I roll to my side and face my grandfather. He's dead serious, and I'm dying to know who the love of his life was.

"Who?" I ask, giddy as a little kid waiting for the end of their favorite bedtime story.

"Your beautiful grandmother," Pops answers matter-of-factly.

"Grandma?" I'm named after her, but I don't know much about her at all. She died before I was born, and neither Pops nor my mom really talk about her. I think it's a little too hard for both of them, even all these years later. "But you're gay," I scoff.

"I'm well aware of that, thank you." A hint of annoyance sneaks into Pops' tone.

"I just mean…"

"You mean you're ignorantly confusing love and sex. Come with me. I want to show you something."

Pops walks to the doorway. When I don't immediately follow, he stomps his cane into the floor three times and chides, "Right now, Jaqueline Marie Ryan. I'm not getting any younger."

With a chuckle, I follow my surly grandfather into his apartment.

"Sit," he commands in an all-too-serious voice.

I do as I'm told for once, taking up residence on his floral loveseat. After a few minutes of rustling sounds emanating from the bedroom, he emerges with an old cigar box and a sad smile. He takes the seat next to me and lovingly strokes the faded crest on the box.

"Did you know your grandmother died slowly, after a long battle with breast cancer?"

I shake my head. I had no idea.

"She had time to plot and she used it wisely. I found this in our safe deposit box with her will the day after she died."

He gingerly opens the cigar box and pulls out an envelope, old enough to be yellowing at the corners. He kisses it reverently before handing it over to me.

My dearest Martin,

I read in a magazine once that the Buddhists believe your soulmate isn't the person who makes your heart race, but the person whom you feel at peace with. That is you, my love. You are my home. My peace. I have treasured every moment of our wonderful life together and I thank you for each day I was able to call you my husband.

But now it's time for you to live your life. To do and see and be all the things you never thought you could. To get you started, I have enclosed a bucket list of sorts. These are all the things you must do for me. And I know you wouldn't dare deny me my dying wish. I'll haunt you and hide your lucky socks.

Darling, I know you are scared, but know you will never be alone. I will always be with you. I will always love you.

The bravest thing you can do with your life is live it how you want. To be who you are. Because you are beautiful.

All my love, now and into eternity,

Your Jackie

P.S. Get started or those socks are history, bud!

With tears building in the corners of my eyes, I turn the page to find the long list of tasks my dying grandmother made for my grandfather. *Ride the New York subway. See a play on Broadway. Kiss a man in Paris. Tour the Louvre. Have afternoon tea in a London cafe. Take drugs in Amsterdam.* Each item is crossed off with a single bold line. The last line at the very bottom of the page reads *Love again.*

The realization hits me with the force of a wrecking ball on a house of cards. "The receipts and memorabilia down in the shop. They were all things you did for her?"

He nods and wipes away a few mournful tears. Taking the letter back, he tucks it in the envelope, kisses it one more time and reverently returns it to the cigar box.

"I loved your grandma more than life itself. We were as different as can be, but she saw me. She knew me, in a way no one else could. She gave me the greatest gift I have ever received. She taught me how to love all of myself, the beautiful and the ugly. The average and the controversial. The bland and the quirky. And for that I will always be grateful to her." He rubs the chain around his neck that holds both of their wedding rings, a sanguine smile on his lips and a wistful look in his mature eyes. "You're named after her, but you are so much like me. We're both so scared of life."

Normally, if someone told me I was scared, I would kick and scream in objection. I would argue until I passed out. But that doesn't feel appropriate surrounded by the memory of my grandmother and her unconditional love for Pops, so I stay quiet and really listen.

"You puff yourself up and pretend to be untouchable, but underneath all the bluster, we are both terrified of not being enough." Pops takes my hand in his and squeezes. "Your grandmother taught me being vulnerable is true strength. Being part of something imperfect is braver than mocking it from the safety of the sidelines."

"I'm so sorry," I admit, feeling like a spoiled brat. "I know you loved her. I wish I could've met her."

"I wish you could've too, kiddo. She would've loved you."

"Does Mom know? About the letter?"

Pops shakes his head.

"Why not? She thinks you abandoned her. You basically orphaned her after Mom died. You know that's why she's mad at you, right?"

"I'd rather her be mad at me than at the memory of her mother. Besides, she has to learn for herself that the secret to happiness is finding more joy being who you are than who you think you are supposed to be."

"I wouldn't hold my breath on that one." I snort.

"I believe in her. Just like I believe in you." Pops wraps an arm around me and pulls me into his side.

"Aww, shucks," I joke, trying to ease the seriousness of the situation with my inappropriate humor.

"Do me a favor, would you?" Pops asks. I hum in affirmation. "Find someone whose love makes you brave. And if you get it wrong, try again. And again.

And again. There is no shame in making the wrong choices to get to the right place."

"Life's about the journey and all that crap?"

"You're such a smart ass."

"Yep. Just like my Pops."

He kisses my forehead and laughs.

Chapter Twenty-Four

Eddie

I take my usual seat in the coffee shop and stare at my phone. I'm too distracted to even pretend to be working. I'm trying to psych myself up before heading upstairs to talk to Jackie, but I feel like I'm volunteering to be the first guy to test out the parachute. She called me her boyfriend then immediately dumped me. *I think.* At least she told me we shouldn't be together. I have no real idea what's going on with her. With us. So I'm sitting here, fiddling with my phone and pretending to check my emails.

"How did things go after your chat with Mama Ryan?" Jesús asks as he sets down the coffee I didn't order but desperately need. I barely slept last night. Strange how my own bed feels foreign — and empty — after spending so many hours in Jackie's.

"Not great." I pinch the bridge of my nose and shake my head.

"I figured not. There's a little something extra in your coffee, *mijo*." He winks and takes the seat next to me. "Those visits always put her in a pissy mood."

"Well, the good news is she finally called me her boyfriend." I take a sip of my tequila with a splash of coffee in it.

Jesús grabs my forearm with both hands and squeezes hard as he squeals. "*Dios mio!* That's amazing."

"Yep. Then she broke up with me. I think."

"You think? Jackie doesn't do subtle. If you were dumped, you'd know it."

His weird reassurance actually makes me feel a bit better. If Jackie didn't want to see me again, she probably would've told me to fuck off and die.

"I'll be honest, JC. I have no fucking idea what she wants."

"Neither does she. She wouldn't know love if it slapped her on that sweet little booty of hers." He blows out a puff of air and waves away my worries. "Look, it took her forever to let me in too, but now? That woman would help me bury a body if I needed, no questions asked. She's like a bucking bronco — you've just got to hold on for those eight seconds. Once you get past all the kicking and screaming, victory is yours."

"And if she kills me in the process?" I run my fingers through my hair, legitimately considering the possibility.

"She won't. She's just scared." Jesús takes a quick look around the coffee shop and lowers his voice to a conspiratorial whisper. "She doesn't trust *any*body at first. Her dad was a philandering asshole who hasn't so much as sent Jackie a birthday card in years. If you ask me, poor Jackie is still trying to figure out what she did wrong."

Suddenly her prickliness makes a bit more sense. *She's waiting for me to get bored and take off.* She thinks that's what people do. Either they judge you like her mother does or they leave you like her father did. A new piece of the beautiful puzzle that is Jaqueline Ryan falls into place.

"Thanks, Jesús."

"Don't mention it. I like you." He gives me a pat on the shoulder with a warm smile and gets back to work.

I make my way up to Jackie's room, still unsure of what to expect. I close my eyes and knock on the door, nerves turning my stomach like a man in front of a firing squad.

"Oh, it's you," she says, answering the door with a small smile. I'm not sure if she's happy to see me, or just surprised.

"It's me," I say with a self-conscious grin, holding my hands up to show I come in peace.

She doesn't invite me in. She just steps away, leaving the door open. I suppose the door not slamming in my face is an invitation in Jackie's world. I step inside and shove my hands in my pockets. She's on the other side of the room, tucking a strand of hair behind her ear and staring into space. We are both standing there, trapped in the awkward silence like it's emotional quicksand.

"Look, I—"

"So I was—" We both start talking at the same time and stop abruptly. We stare at each other again for a long moment.

"You were saying—?"

"I was just going—"

We start and stop again. The silence engulfs us once more. The tension is up to my mouth, about to steal my breath when Jackie rolls her eyes and shouts, "For fuck's sake. I'm *sorry*, okay. I was an asshole. Can we just move on now?"

I stare at her, completely baffled.

"What?" She crosses her arms, annoyed with me. I can't help but let out a surprised snort.

"Give me a minute. Jackie Ryan just apologized to me. I need to re-evaluate my understanding of the universe." I hold my index fingers up by my temples and twirl them in little loops like the wheels are turning.

She cracks a smile, although she is clearly trying really damn hard not to. Her lips pucker up in a weird pout as a result, and I bust out laughing. Jackie charges over to me and gives me a playful shove.

"You're such an asshole. I'm standing here, being the magnanimous one, and you're laughing your dorky little ass off."

"Sorry. I'm sorry." I steel my features and reach out for her. "Apology accepted. Thank you very much." I cup her face with my hands and stare into those fiery eyes. "Seriously, thank you."

I lean down and place a gentle kiss on her soft lips.

"Don't get used to it. I'm not planning on making a habit of it. Now I need you to strip me naked and mount me like a golden retriever on a stuffed teddy bear. I hear make-up sex is ah-MAZ-ing."

"I think I can make that happen."

I wrap my arms around Jackie and pull her in to me. Holding her tight, I slide my fingers into her fiery hair. Just before our desperate mouths connect, I still. I revel in the charge building between our eager bodies. She moans and teases me with a nip at my lower lip. She'll bitch about it, but she loves when I hold back. Taunting her is the best foreplay.

Just when she starts to pull away, I attack, assaulting her perfect lips and invading her sumptuous mouth. I kiss her deep and long, until I've purged every ounce of the terror and insecurity that had been building inside me since I last saw her. My kiss leaves no doubt. I've fallen hard for this woman and there's no turning back now.

Chapter Twenty-Five

Jackie

"So, where are you taking me for our first date?" I flip down the visor on Eddie's very sensible Ford Focus and check my scarlet lipstick. *Fierce as ever.* I smile at my reflection and snap the mirror closed.

"Dinner and a movie," Eddie answers.

I let out a long, low groan. "Seriously, Khakis? I didn't think you could get more *blah* but once again, you have outdone yourself."

"Oh, shut up. You think my consistency is dead sexy." His voice takes that raspy, bossy tone that makes hot desire pool in my stomach.

"Sexy consistency makes about as much sense as a combination magic show and gynecological exam." I wave my hands around, mimic reaching into a *hole* and pulling out a string of scarves. "Wow, they just keep coming. Don't worry, we've got an ointment for that. Honk. Honk." I pretend to squeeze a clown nose.

Eddie throws his head back and laughs. The comforting sound fills his small car and makes me feel warm all over.

"You're in fine form tonight."

"I didn't get my nap today.

"Oh, I'm sorry. I didn't realize you were a toddler."

"Fuck you," I shoot back in a playful pout.

He laughs again, and I wonder why we're bothering to go anywhere when I've got a perfectly good empty bed back in my apartment.

He clicks a button on his watch, and it makes a loud beep. "Five minutes and twenty-three seconds into our first real date and you're already swearing at me. Not bad. Not great. But not bad," he teases.

"Whatever. You know you love it. You're my little submissive, Khakis." Funny enough, in bed is where he likes to take charge the most. And I have to say I'm happy to let him. The man knows his way around a vagina!

"I like a girl who can give it as good as she gets," he says using his bossy-raspy tone again.

This time, instead of letting the sound tingle my girlie bits, I decide to screw with him.

I lean across the center console of the car, lower my voice conspiratorially and say, "So, you're into the whole *strap-on* thing? I mean, I've always wanted to try…" I let my words trail off. Without breaking my stare, I give a quick suggestive fist pump in the air. "Pegging."

The look of sheer horror on his face is priceless.

"Oh, God, no," he finally exclaims, and I crack up laughing.

"Don't worry, Khakis. I'm just fucking with you."

He lets out a sigh, but even in the darkness of the car I can tell he's smirking.

"We're here," he announces and turns off the engine.

"Where is here exactly?" I look around at the abandoned factories and warehouses. Not the cloth napkins and waiters in tuxedos I was expecting.

"Dinner." He gets out of the car, comes around to my side and opens the door, because he's a dork. And also, a gentleman.

"And what's for dessert? A tetanus shot?" I quip as I let him help me out of the car.

The large, pothole-laden parking lot is nearly empty, but the handful of cars that are here don't seem abandoned. Instead, they look new and expensive. It is dark with just a single flickering streetlight illuminating the large area, so it is hard to tell, but I swear one of them is a Ferrari. The smell of rusting machinery and old oil still permeates the air, but underneath there is a sweetness I can't put my finger on. We walk up to some creaky old door, and Eddie gives it three loud raps. I'm expecting to see rats scurry out from under it, but instead a young guy in an all-white outfit opens it with a huge smile.

"Welcome to Crashing Dinner. Right this way."

The guy leads us down a long concrete hallway, up a flight of rickety stares and, finally, into a massive warehouse. Except tonight it isn't a warehouse. Tonight, it is a ballroom. There is a red carpet leading to several small tables. Each is decked out with crisp linens, copious amounts of silverware, and a single red rose in a crystal vase. From the rafters, long dangling strings of dancing lights illuminate the space with a surprisingly cozy glow. A string quartet plays softly on one of the overhangs. Several couples are swaying on the small dance floor in the corner while other couples chat at their own intimate tables.

I study the place, amazed at how something so mundane can be so beautiful. The venue is charming because it is so unexpected. I'm smiling from ear to ear when I finally turn back to look at Eddie who is now seated across from me at our table for two.

"Aren't you full of surprises?"

Eddie beams with pride so I bury my head in the menu to ignore him. We order our food and stare at each other for a minute. I've been naked on top of him, but somehow this feels more intimate. Certainly more romantic.

"Is this where we're supposed to make cutesy small talk?" I ask, hoping to deflect some of my unease.

"It is. In fact..." Eddie reaching into his jacket pocket and pulls out a tiny book. I can just make out the *Conversation Starters* written on the cover.

"Oh God, kill me now." I'm overly dramatic and it doesn't give Eddie a minute's pause.

"Do you believe in the afterlife?" he asks.

"Sure."

"Really?" He reels, clearly surprised.

"Not because I want to go to heaven. Because I love picturing certain people in hell," I clarify.

He flips the page and asks, "What is your biggest dream?"

My gaze dances around the room as I think. There's really only one answer. "Winning the E.B. Jericho cover contest. Becoming a world-renowned, much-sought-after graphic designer, and never making another cup of coffee for the rest of my life."

"It's really that big of a deal to you?" His voice is soft, almost like he's afraid of the answer.

"It would only completely change my life." I shrug.

"I don't get it. Then why haven't you ever entered?"

"I will."

"When?"

"Soon." I shift in my seat, suddenly feeling like I'm under interrogation now.

"When is that?"

"When I'm ready."

"So, never?"

"Why are you being an ass? Can you just drop it?" I snap at him right when our waiter shows up with the first course.

"Fine. Consider it dropped."

Dinner is a little stiff and hostile. Eddie tries a couple times to get me to talk, but I'm in a sour mood now.

"I'm sorry, okay?" Eddie says after we finish up and are heading back out to the car. "I just think if that's your dream, you should go for it. You've got the talent."

He opens the door for me, and I stand on the other side of it, waiting to get in. I take a minute to study him. His mouth is turned down at the corners, his eyebrows are pinched together, and his forehead is wrinkled. Eddie's contrition face is pretty adorable.

"Thanks," I whisper and give him a soft kiss before climbing into his car.

Chapter Twenty-Six

Jackie

I wipe away the steam from my shower and take a long look at myself in the mirror. My bright red hair is darker while it's wet, my cheeks soft pink thanks to the three orgasms Eddie just coaxed out of me and my make-up free face looks fresh and innocent. A string of pearls and one of Elizabeth's conservative dresses, and I might actually look like Eddie's girlfriend. *Almost.* Until I open my mouth.

I throw my hair up in a messy bun, spikey bits hanging out in every direction. I slip on a large black Nine Inch Nails T-shirt with the collar cut wide so that it slips off one shoulder, revealing an appalling amount of cleavage. A coat of Devil May Care red lipstick, and I smile at my new reflection. *That's more like it.* I'm nobody's sweetheart.

I stroll out to the bedroom, basking in the warm caress that is Eddie's lingering gaze on my bare legs. I cross the room to my desk with no purpose other than to torture him with the sway of my hips. There's a reason I'm wearing an oversized T-shirt and nothing else. *I'm a naughty girl.*

I sort through the chaos on my desk, pretending to have had a reason to saunter across the room. On top of the normal pile of randomness is a sketch pad. It is the exact same one I have been using for months, but it can't be. That one is in the trash, the pages used up and torn out. I haven't gotten around to replacing it. I just keep doodling in the corners and on the back of old drawings.

"What's this?" I ask Khakis and hold up the mysterious new arrival.

"A sketch pad," he deadpans, naked in my bed.

"Thanks, smartass. I mean, what is it doing here?" I cock out a hip and furrow my brow.

"I saw yours was almost empty last week, so I grabbed a new one. Oh, and these." He reaches into his messenger bag leaning up against my milkcrate nightstand and pulls out a box of Sakura Pigma Micron pens — my absolute favorite. He walks across the room and hands them to me with an innocent smile despite being naked.

I stare down at the small gesture, and I'm overcome with the simple sincerity of it. It's not extravagant, but it is amazingly considerate, which is worth so much more. Not only did he take the time to know me and what I like, he believes in my art enough to make sure I can keep making it. I don't know that anyone has done anything so sweet for me in a *long* time. I pull my quivering lip into my mouth and bite down to keep from getting choked up. *Get a grip, Jackie. It's just a damn sketch pad!*

"They're the right kind, aren't they?" Eddie asks, running a hand through his hair. He's mistaking my overwhelmed reaction with disappointment. "I thought they were what you use, but if you don't like them—"

"They're perfect." I toss the pad and pens on my desk and throw my arms around this ridiculous man. "You're perfect, you colossal dork."

The goofy smile on his face tugs at the strings of my heart hard enough I can feel it down to my toes.

I'm in trouble. I'm falling in love with a pair of khakis.

* * * *

I slide my hands down my vintage-style green dress with soft pink polka dots and try not to vomit. Eddie will be here any minute to pick me up. I've known for a month that his mom's dinner party was coming, like a tsunami barreling down and promising to wash away any stupid ideas I have about Eddie and I actually making this work. We're too different. I know it and deep down he must know it too.

"This is stupid." I shake my head at the image of myself on my computer screen.

"You look beautiful." Elizabeth's voice rings through my speakers. "Like a young Mae West with attitude."

"Who the hell is Mae West?"

"Only like *the* quintessential pinup girl! The inventor of the hourglass figure."

"I look like a poser." I pick at the cutesy bow cinching in the tiniest part of my waist.

"You look like a woman in *looooove,*" Austin chimes in from over Elizabeth's shoulder, drawing out the nasty four-letter word.

"Fuck off, Man Meat," I snap back while flipping him the bird.

"That's not a denial." He taps the side of his nose with his index finger like some cliché mafioso in a cheesy mob movie.

"Jackie!" Elizabeth squeals with excitement, ever the optimist. "Are you in love?"

"What the hell do you think?" I deflect.

"I think I've never seen you try this hard with anyone else."

"Yeah, well, he's got a nice cock," I deadpan.

"Jackie," Elizabeth admonishes me, saying my name with the disappointed tone of a kindergarten teacher catching a kid with a mouthful of paste.

"I've gotta go. He'll be here soon."

As if on cue, Eddie's telltale *rat-a-tat-tat* knock has me crawling me out of my skin.

"Have fun," Elizabeth sings with a sweet smile.

"Be safe," Austin adds with a lascivious smirk that leaves no doubt he's talking about fucking.

"Right back at you two, you crazy kids. Don't try any positions I wouldn't." I blow them both a kiss and end the video chat.

"Holy cow," Eddie exclaims when I open the door. His hungry eyes take in every inch of me. In addition to the dress, my hair is up in a wavy bun, minimizing the in-your-face-ness of the red color and my makeup is all soft natural colors.

"Watch it," I warn, holding up a finger. "The next words to come out of your mouth will determine if you will ever be able to father children."

Eddie shoves his hands into his pockets, shakes his head and chuckles. Apparently, my threats have lost their power.

"You look absolutely stunning, as usual," he answers, dipping to kiss me on the cheek. He offers me his arm like a true gentleman. "Shall we?"

"Fuck it. Sure."

Eddie's mom's house is only about a half-hour drive, but it might as well be on another planet. Unlike my cozy studio apartment in the heart of downtown, Eddie's mom lives deep in the suburbs. Her house isn't as extravagant as I thought it would be. While the house is the nicest on the block, it isn't exactly a mansion. More upper-middle-class than the one percent. I side-eye Eddie, my curiosity about what he does for a living rekindled.

"So this is home sweet home?" I ask when he parks in the long driveway. Everything about Khakis is bland, meant to blend in to the background flawlessly, his beige car included. Would a red convertible kill him?

"Nah, this is just my mom's house. I didn't grow up here or anything. I've never even spent the night here."

"Because you lived with your grandma?" I ask, bring up his previous confession about his childhood.

Coming around to my side of the car, Eddie takes my hand to help me out. It's a good thing too because I'm dangerous in heels on a good day and the paving stones that lead the way to the house are perilous.

"Yep. Because we used to live with my grandma. I guess I'd call her place home if anything. I bought this place for Mom with my first big bonus."

We've made our way up to the front door, but Eddie pauses before walking in, as if he is begging me to ask the question. I won't give him the satisfaction, regardless of how badly I want to know what he does. Asking ruins the game. It's admitting defeat.

"As a multi-million-dollar home realtor?" I ask.

He shakes his head, staring at our hands. He gently strokes the back of my hand with his thumb and says, "Wrong again, Ignis."

I narrow my eyes on him and rub my chin with my free hand. I study him for a quick moment.

"Fixer for the rich and famous?" I tease. "You're the guy everyone comes to when they want to leak a sex tape!"

"You got it! Amateur pornography is my calling," Eddie says flatly. He closes his eyes and places a hand on his chest in reverence.

My jaw drops, and I stare at him. It's unbelievable, but it also makes sense. It's always the quiet ones that keep the biggest secrets. Plus, he's *amazing* in bed. And he clearly has money and sets his own schedule. *Holy cow, my boyfriend is a porn producer!*

"Calm down. That was a joke," Eddie adds quickly with a furrowed brow. He rings the doorbell, a long echoing chime.

"I knew you weren't that cool," I say under my breath.

"Only you would be disappointed about that." There's a hit of amusement in his tone.

"A lifetime of free porn slipped between my fingers." I hold up a fist, pretend to give a blow job with a tongue in my cheek before slowly opening my palm and blowing away the lost erotica.

And because the universe hates me, it is that exact moment that Eddie's mom decides to open the door to greet us. With me talking about porn and miming a blowie. The scandalized look on her face tells me she does not appreciate the conversation.

"Good evening, Mom." Eddie tries to recover by acting like it didn't happen. "I'd like you to meet my girlfriend, Jackie."

I unlatch my hand from Eddie's and hold it out to her. She shakes just the tips of my fingers, as if she's trying not to touch the soiled girl.

"Charmed," she drawls. She steps aside, and we enter the lion's den. "Everyone is in the drawing room for appetizers and cocktails. Dinner is at six-thirty."

Eddie, smart man that he is, leads me over to the bar set up in the corner of the large *drawing room*. She means living room without a television. I see no purpose for this room short of having people standing around in it and gossip. Seems like a waste. I could set up a sweet game room in here. Big screen on the far wall, four or five gaming chairs, surround sound, mini-fridge and a wet bar. Now, that would be a party. *A girl can dream.*

"Here you go." Eddie hands me a whiskey neat, and I'm trying to remember when I mentioned that was my favorite drink.

"Thanks." I take it from him eagerly. My palms are sweaty and my skin is itchy. I tell myself, again, that what these people think of me doesn't matter. I look up at Eddie, and his self-conscious smile, and know that what *he* thinks of me matters.

"Sorry about my mom," Eddie says to me in a low whisper. "She can be a bit much."

"I noticed." I take a long pull of my whiskey, the robust liquid burning down my throat.

"She's always cared too much about what people think."

"And you don't?" I scoff. I could use confirmation right now that this isn't a test, because I'm going to fail. Harder than Eddie up on that stage in drag.

"I don't—" Eddie doesn't get to finish before his mom waves him over. "I'll be right back."

Based on the wild hand gestures, something has gone wildly amiss in Mrs. Jaworski's world. Eddie shrugs a few times before the glare his mother is leveling at him hits home. With a quick, annoyed step, he crosses the room back to me.

"I've got to head to the store. Apparently, I was supposed to bring the cinnamon sticks for the hot toddy garnish. And it's her *signature* drink. I've gotta run out and grab them real quick before there is a world-ending meltdown."

"Sounds like quite an emergency," I tease, despite the sick feeling in my stomach at the thought of being left to solo this dinner-party extravaganza. "Need a co-pilot?"

"Much as I love having you as my partner in crime, it'll be faster if I go alone. I'll be back as soon as I can. I promise." Eddie gives me a quick kiss on my cheek before heading for the door.

I've never wanted to call out after a man so bad in my life. Panic dumps through my body like a poison. I finish my whiskey and remind myself I'm a strong, independent woman who will not be intimidated by a bunch of white-collar stiffs.

I stride up to Eddie's mom, her lively chat with a friend coming to a quick end.

"I wanted to say thank you for the invitation to your party." I plaster on my best fake smile, trying harder than I'd like to admit to get a woman I don't particularly like to approve of me.

"Of course, dear. Any friend of Eddie's..." she trails off. It riles me up something fierce.

"Girlfriend," I correct her. I've never claimed that title so fervently in all my life.

"Right," she answers with her own fake smile.

"The graphic designer?" her friend asks. He is older, probably in his late sixties, rocking a tweed jacket and salt and pepper hair. He looks like a college economics professor.

"Actually, I'm just a barista in my grandfather's coffee shop," I correct him too. I'm as much a graphic designer as I am an astronaut. I'd have to get paid for my work at some point to call myself a graphic designer.

"I thought Eddie said he was dating a graphic designer. My apologies. Being an old man sometimes gets the better of me."

"Will you excuse me," I croak out. I search the large house for a bathroom and lock myself in. I need to think.

Eddie lied about me. *Of course he lied.* Who would admit to dating a wild redheaded coffee wench? He didn't even invite me here, his grandmother did. And he's too damn polite to ever *un*invite me, no matter how ashamed of me he is. The crippling insecurity I usually bury too deep to feel crawls out of the hole I shoved it into and clutches my throat in a suffocating grip.

I'm out of here.

I don't bother saying goodbye to anyone. I make a mad dash to the front door. I'll call a rideshare when I'm out of here, I just need to get some air first. I skirt around the living room, the growing crowd too distracted with small talk to notice my freak out.

In my hurry to escape, I slip on the paving stones without Eddie's help.

"Fuck!" I shout as I faceplant into the rocks.

"Jackie, are you all right?" a soft voice calls out across the driveway. I push myself up to meet the concerned face of Evelyn, Eddie's grandmother.

"I'm fine. Just thought I saw a penny. A girl can use any good luck she can find."

"Especially facing a night with my daughter," she answers with a knowing smile. "Where's Eddie?"

"On the hunt for cinnamon sticks."

Evelyn rolls her eyes. "That woman loves her garnishes. If I hadn't carried her for nine months, I'd swear she wasn't mine."

I let out a low laugh. Gingerly standing up, I brush off my dress and give Evelyn a forced smile.

"Did she chase you away?" She reaches for my hand and squeezes.

"Those marshmallows? Girlie, please." *Kind of.* "I just need to get back to the shop. Coffee emergency." Yes, that is a lame excuse and yes, we both know it's bullshit. Still, Evelyn has enough class not to call me out on the lie.

"What do you want me to tell Eddie?"

"Just that I…just tell him to have fun."

I'm in the back of an Uber, heading to the safety of my apartment before I can think twice about how bad it hurts to run away.

Chapter Twenty-Seven

Eddie

I am out of breath, practically running through the grocery store and back to the house. My stomach is doing barrel rolls and my head is churning with a million ways the night can go, most of them quite horrible. Sometimes having an overactive imagination is really unhelpful.

Handing off the godforsaken cinnamon sticks, I ask my mom, "Where's Jackie?" I didn't see her on my way in.

"I'm not sure. I haven't seen her in a while," she answers while rifling through the shopping bag.

"What do you mean you haven't seen her? I asked you to look after her. She doesn't know anyone here."

"Really, darling. I'm hosting a party here. I can't babysit your friend at the expense of my other guests."

"My *girl*friend, and you damn well should've tried."

"Language, Edwin!"

I shoulder past my mother and start my search for Jackie. She's not in the drawing room or the dining room. I check both downstairs bathrooms. Still no luck. My grandmother waves me down when I double back to the drawing room.

"Grandma, have you seen Jackie?" I kneel in front of her where she's sitting on the couch.

"She left." She tsks with disappointment.

"What?" I shout, drawing more than a few concerned looks and a glare from my mom. "When?"

"About twenty minutes ago. She said to tell you to have fun, as if this is the time for that sort of nonsense. I have a feeling her leaving had to do with her being abandoned."

"I was only gone a few minutes!" I raise my voice again, not giving a shit about my mom's party. "Mom had to have her damn garnish."

I let out a low groan, not sure who I'm more annoyed with, my mom or my girlfriend.

Grandma smacks me on the shoulder.

"Priorities, for heaven's sake, child! I told you not to lose that one," she chides, reminding me what she whispered in my ear at my brunch with Jackie a few weeks ago.

"I know. I'm trying. She doesn't make it easy."

"Good things rarely are." She nods in that older, wiser way grandparents do.

"Yes, Grandma." I kiss her on the temple and head back out to my car. I've been playing this game with Jackie for too long for her to balk now.

As I climb behind the wheel, my mind races with a million possibilities of what will happen when I find Jackie. I navigate the turns to the shop without a thought, as if driven by a larger fate. The whole drive,

I'm consumed by calculating with the best way to handle my hurt and frustration. I'm parked in front of Beans & Dreams before I've come up with an answer.

I take the steps to her apartment two at a time and pound on her door. I'm out of breath and my heart is racing. I'm trying to control my anger at being ghosted without much success.

"Where the hell did you go?" I snarl when she opens the door, before she even has a chance to say hello. I shove my way into the apartment. She backs away, letting me in, but doesn't take her angry glare off me. She's in ripped black jeans and a loose T-shirt that says *Video games don't make me violent. Lag does.* The bright red lipstick I love is back on her luscious lips. She looks like herself again.

"Away from you. Thought that was obvious."

"I can see that." I slam the door behind me and cross my arms. "Mind telling me why? What did I do this time?" I try not to think about how much I love her and how scared I am that she'll burn our relationship to the ground before it even starts. *Again.*

"Hmmm, let me think." She taps her chin with her index finger ironically before snapping, "First you abandon me, then I find out you lied about me. I'm not ashamed of who I am and I'm not going to be with someone who is."

"I was gone all of ten minutes and what exactly did I lie about? I'm not ashamed of anything and I honestly have no idea what you're talking about."

"You told some old guy that I am a graphic designer." She flails her arms wide like she's trying to backhand me from across the room.

"You are." I shrug, still not understanding.

"Funny, because the last time I checked my pay stub comes from a coffee shop."

"Slinging coffee is what you do. A graphic designer is what you are."

"Oh, I get it. You're not lying. You're just using alternative facts that sound more impressive for my sake."

"Look, I don't give a shit what anyone at that party thinks. They're just my mom's friends, and frankly, a bunch of twats. And I didn't lie. You're an artist, regardless of the fact that you're too scared to show your work to anyone."

She stomps her foot on the floor hard enough the full-length mirror leaning against the wall behind her slides down to the floor with a clang.

"Hey, asshole. I'm not scared of anything." She points a finger at me, her eyes wide and wild.

"Bullshit. You're terrified of letting someone judge your designs. And you're terrified of letting me get too close."

"I'll submit my work when I'm good and ready, not when some tight-ass pressures me into it. And please, I eat guys like you for lunch."

"Then why did you run from a dinner party tonight?"

"Because I'm not this person." She crosses to the bed, swipes her dress off the bed and throws it in my face. "I can't be what you want and I'm not going to try."

"What are you talking about? I'm not asking you to be anything."

"Yes, you are. With your button-down shirts and pressed pants! With your brunches and your dinner parties. You're asking me to be this put-together person. And that's not me. I can't wake up one morning and decide to be an adult. Like suddenly I'm going to start eating my vegetables, doing my laundry and paying taxes."

"Okay, we'll circle back to the paying-taxes thing, because the federal government isn't asking. But, for the rest of it, I don't need you to *be* anything or anyone. If you want those things for yourself, great. You just have to wake up every morning and try."

"You're saying I'm not trying? I work my ass off!"

"No, you're hiding. From a leap you're too scared to take behind a job you hate." I run my fingers through my hair and tug at the ends. This woman drives me absolutely insane. "Life isn't all or nothing. Some days will be shit, and you'll have ice cream for dinner. Others, you'll actually iron something. Succeed or fail, trying is what counts. That's the real secret to being an adult. You just keep fucking trying."

"And if I can't?"

"Then you can't. So what?"

"So, one of these days you're going to wake up next to a grown woman in footie pajamas with a taco sauce stain and wonder what the hell you're doing. One day you're going to get sick of it and just stop loving me." She is screaming at me, but tears are building in her eyes and there is a new fragility to her voice. Her chest is rising and falling as she pants in a near panic.

I take a minute to let her truth settle on me. It's more than being too scared of failing to bother trying. She's terrified of standing in front of someone she cares about and not being good enough.

"Jackie, listen to me. The only way that is going to happen is if you don't share those tacos," I joke to ease the tension as I slowly get closer.

"Fuck off. Tacos are life," she volleys back, a little bit of that ferociousness I love coming back to her.

"I think you are amazing. Exactly as you are. You're smart and funny. Loyal and strong. Sweet—when you're in the mood to be—and the sexiest woman I've ever been lucky enough to lay my hands on. I'm not saying you don't annoy the hell out of me sometimes, but I promise, I will never just walk away."

I reach out and pull her into me. She slides her arms around my waist, squeezes me hard and buries her face in my chest. I rub her back in long soothing stokes, hoping it's enough to get her past the fear.

"Besides, who says I'll ever fall in love with you anyway?" I tease to bring her back to her snarky comfort zone.

"Oh, please. You've been in love with me since day one," she scoffs. She throws her head back and smiles up at me.

"You're right. That espresso garnish was impossible to resist." I tuck a strand of her soft hair behind her ear, cup her face and place a gentle kiss on her full lips.

"I've been busting my ass to chase you away," she admits on a long exhale.

"I noticed." I hum in acknowledgment.

"Awww," she coos and pokes me in the ribs. "And here I thought you were completely oblivious."

"Well, in all honesty I may be a little blind when it comes to you." I brush her soft, pink cheek with my thumb and stare deep into those hazel eyes. I hold my breath just before telling her, "Because I'm in love with you."

With a sly smile, she rises on her tiptoes to kiss me. "Told you so."

I let out a low groan.

She pulls back, looking me in the eyes when she admits on a soft whisper, "I love you too."

I claim her mouth in a soul-stealing kiss. I slide my tongue into her eager mouth and taste the victory of being able to call this woman mine.

Chapter Twenty-Eight

Eddie

"Congrats, man," Ben tells me with a slap on the shoulder.

"What are you congratulating him for? He's behind his deadline," Darla asks as she stalks into Ben's office with purpose. The woman has never *strolled* anywhere in her life.

The congratulations are a bit out of order since this is supposed to be my writer's intervention. Darla and Ben are not my friends right now, but my agent and my editor. They're going to sit me down and tell me I need to finish my next book, or I'll be in breach of contract and have some steep penalties to pay the publisher.

"Haven't you heard? Eddie's in love," Ben answers with genuine joy in his voice.

"Fuck," Darla says with a huff as she collapses into the seat next to me. "Well, we're up shit creek. Benji, get me a drink."

"Sure thing, boss," Ben mocks, but pulls out the bottle of brandy he keeps in his desk anyway and pours her a tall glass. It is usually reserved for celebratory toasts, but it'll be better for all three of us if Darla takes the edge off.

"It'll be fine." I try to convince the both of them for the millionth time that I can do two things at once. I can be in love with Jackie and meet my deadline. *I hope.*

"Oh really? Good to know. Care to tell me how?"

"I've been writing."

"Is the book finished?"

"No—"

"Then we're fucked." She downs the brandy in one long swig.

"Darla," Ben tries to chime in, but gets shot down.

"This is the long-awaited, much *publicized* last book in the Persei Rivera series."

"I'm well aware of that. I did write the damn things," I snap. Jackie's attitude is starting to rub off on me.

"Don't get snippy with me, mister. Right now I'm the only thing standing between you and a breach-of-contract lawsuit. The publisher is going to be pissed! A lot of money has gone into prepping for this launch. We can't just turn it off."

"I get that. I'll make the deadline."

"Sure you will." She stands, hands Ben the empty glass and struts to the door.

"Where are you going?" Ben asks.

"To save our asses and beg for an extension."

"You're the best," I call to her. I don't have to turn around to know she's wearing her sour face and shaking her head.

"You're paying for this. *Literally*," she chides before making her exit.

"That went better than expected. You're still alive." Ben chuckles and hands me a shot of tequila he keeps around just for me since I hate brandy. We clink glasses and down the liquor. "Seriously though, you need to buckle down and get this done."

"I know. I will." But instead of plotting my next Chapter like my mind usually does in every spare minute while I'm writing a book, my thoughts drift to the soft skin and sharp wit of the woman I can't get enough of. Jackie is both a distraction and an inspiration. If only I could figure out how to balance the two.

Ben tilts his head and narrows his eyes at me like he doesn't quite believe me. I don't blame him. I'm not very convinced I can put Jackie on the back burner either. Regardless, he shakes it off and changes the subject. Benji's never been good at being a nag. I pay Darla for that.

"So, how did Jackie react when she found out?"

"That I'm in love with her? I think she knew before I did." I laugh. It's not like I've tried to hide my feelings. It's been pretty obvious I'm fascinated with Jackie since day one. Apparently, fascination is a stepping-stone to love.

"No shit, *everyone* knew before you did. I meant when she found out you're E.B. Jericho."

I stare down at my shoes, swallow hard and clear my throat. The guilt of not having come clean to Jackie yet weighs on me like a ton of bricks.

"Wait, don't tell me she still doesn't know?" Ben admonishes me. I don't answer. "Edwin Bartlett Jaworski, that poor woman is in love with you. She needs to know the truth!" Ben twists the knife of guilt lodged in my heart. I know he's right and a thick layer of shame coats my guilt in an impenetrable blackness.

"I never meant to lie to her," I mumble. "It all started out as a game. This stupid bet to see if she could guess what I do."

Ben crosses his arms and stares at me, calling me a liar without a word.

"Okay, yeah, I didn't want to lead with the whole *I'm your favorite author* thing. You know how people act when they find out. They change. Every relationship turns weirdly transactional. Suddenly it's about what I can do for them rather than who I am. But I *was* going to tell her. I was just waiting for the right time."

"Which for the record, should've been before you fucked her and *definitely* before she fell in love with you."

"Benji, I know. Trust me, I know. But it happened so fast. Then, we were more than friends, but not really together. And she's skittish. It's like she's always looking for a reason to push me away." I drop my head into my hands in my lap. "Now, it's so late."

"Yep."

"It's going to be a big deal," I whine into my palms, the words garbled.

"Yep."

"And she's going to be pissed." I let out a long, pained sigh. It's not Jackie's anger I'm afraid of, although I will be sure to keep sharp objects out of arm's reach. It's the chance of losing her that terrifies me. It's taken so long to tear down her walls. I'm just now starting to get glimpses of the real her and once she finds out I've been keeping a massive secret? She's going to lock away her heart behind barbed wire and a minefield.

"Oh, hell yes," Benji answers, handing me a second shot of tequila.

"Any suggestions?" I down the shot.

"Do it now. The longer you wait the harder it's going to be."

I drop my head back against the chair and stare up at his office ceiling. "I just walk up to her and say it? Jackie, I'm E.B. Jericho. I meant to tell you earlier, but you know, I was really enjoying the sex and didn't want you to put my balls in the coffee grinder."

Ben snorts at my side. "Coffee grinder? Come on man, she's intense for sure, but she's not Hannibal Lecter."

"Trust me, Ben. If you don't hear from me again, check the coffee grinder."

* * * *

I was up all night, racking my brain, thinking through a million different versions of telling Jackie. I've basically been lying to her since we met. Forty-nine and a half percent of them end with her inflicting some sort of bodily harm before dumping me unceremoniously. Forty-nine and a half of them end with her breaking down into tears and never speaking to me again, which is so much worse. The last one percent, aliens invade, and she forgives me in order to form a united front against the slimy invaders. My imagination isn't always an asset.

I told Jackie I needed to stay at my place tonight to get some work done. Which is true. I *really* need to write. But I can't. All I can do is picture the furious look on her face when I tell her. The hateful words that are going to spill from her beautiful mouth. I can't even think of a good way to bring it up. I was hinting at it on my mom's doorstep, telling her I got a big commission bonus, hoping she'd outright ask me, and we could put it behind us. Unfortunately, that conversation went sideways on me. Leave it to Jackie to make everything about porn. *Damn, I'm going to miss that woman.*

Thinking of ways to tell her without having to actually *tell* her, I get a brilliant idea. Instagram. Maybe if I drop enough clues, she'll straight up ask. I can pretend like I wasn't hiding it, just didn't get around to telling her. Like it's not a big deal. It might be the alcohol and the lack of sleep, but I can't see any flaws in this plan.

I pull up the photo I took on my phone of her mural in the coffee shop, Persei looking kickass and indestructible. Without thinking about it too much—courtesy of the tequila Ben got me started with and the beers that have been keeping me going—I post the picture on E.B. Jericho's Instagram. I'm surprised I even remember the account password. I almost never post stuff myself since my publicist takes care of all my Jericho accounts, but desperate times call for extreme measures.

I chug the rest of my beer followed by a glass of water to preemptively fight tomorrow's hangover before crawling into my big empty bed. I get a restless night's sleep before facing my fate at the hands of a tumultuous redhead.

Chapter Twenty-Nine

Jackie

"Are you hungover?" I ask Eddie when he walks into Beans & Dreams, rubbing his temples and wearing sunglasses despite the overcast weather. He told me he had to "work" last night, and apparently that involved the free flow of alcohol. Maybe he's a poker player. I snicker at the thought of my strait-laced Khakis in his button-down pushing his chips all in at the high-stakes table.

"Coffee?" he croaks out.

I take pity on the poor guy and bring him a dark roast, a bottle of water and two aspirin.

"Drink up, we need to talk."

He takes his sunglasses off and his eyes are bloodshot. He smiles nervously at me, but I don't put him out of his misery. After polishing off his bottle of water, he looks at me like a condemned man and mutters, "Okay. I'm ready."

I pull out my phone and hand it to him. He looks down at the screen, open to my Instagram account. His eyes pinch closed, and he frowns. *That hangover must be pretty brutal.*

"Look, I know I should've—" Eddie starts, but I don't have time for his apologies for one stupid night of drinking too much. Hell, we've all had to crawl from the toilet bowl into the shower at some point in our lives. Besides, he looks like he's suffering enough already. I'm not a sadist.

"E.B. Jericho, *the* E.B. Jericho likes my work!" I blurt out. I can't control the giant smile on my face. I've been practically vibrating with excitement since I woke up this morning. "She posted my mural on her Instagram and it already has ten thousand likes."

"Really? That can't be right," Eddie mutters under his breath and studies the image on my phone.

"Excuse you," I snatch my phone and pull away. "I get that you're feeling pretty rough, but that's no reason to be shitty."

"No, I didn't mean it like that. I'm sorry." He grabs my wrist and leads me back down to the bench seat next to him. "Your mural is amazing. I just mean that account never gets that kind of engagement."

I study him for a quick moment, deciding if I want to be pissed, or if his apology is enough. *Screw it.* I'm too happy to be mad right now.

"It's crazy, right? My mural is going viral! She never posts anything personal, just book news and release promos and stuff, so people are going nuts over it. Plus, she didn't remove the metadata from the image, so now everyone's trying to be the first one to figure out who she is."

"Wait, what?" Eddie nearly does a spit take. Choking back his hot coffee, he starts coughing.

"Did Ben talk you into dropping acid or something? What's up with you today?"

He is acting really weird, which for him is saying a lot. His picture is posted in the dictionary next to the word mundane.

"I'm fine. Just didn't get much sleep." He wipes off the coffee dribbling down his chin and asks, "What's metadata?"

"It's the code your phone puts on every photo you take with a timestamp and location. I know she was here, in this shop on January eighteenth at nine twenty-seven. Which is kind of weird because she was here months ago and just posted the photo—"

"You can do that?" Eddie jumps in. "I thought only like the FBI can do that sort of thing."

"Nah, It's stupid easy. There are even websites set up to do it for you. If you're computer illiterate, all you need is a credit card." With every word Eddie turns more and more pale. "Anyway, the point is she was *here*. In my cafe."

"Coffee shop," he corrects me. I'm too excited to care.

"Whatever. I must have *seen* her. And I'm kicking myself that I only remember this obnoxious woman in a pants suit. It couldn't be her though. Could it?" I muse aloud. It's a rhetorical question, but Eddie looks like he's struggling for the right answer.

"So, all of this got me thinking." I take a long breath, press my lips together to hold it in until I can't stand it and scream, "I'm entering the contest."

His eyes go wide, and he stares at me blankly. He's in shock. I was too. It took me a few hours and a few dozen confirmations from everyone I know to realize that my favorite author posted a picture of *my* mural! I've been double-checking the post every fifteen minutes since I first saw it. But it's real. And this is my moment, I can feel it.

"Really?" Eddie asks incredulously.

"Really. I mean it this time. If E.B. Jericho herself likes my mural enough to post it on Instagram, I've got to have at least half a chance, right?" I bite my lip and stare at him. I'm ashamed to say how important his support means to me right now.

"Absolutely. I think that's amazing. And I know you're going to win." He gives me a small smile, although it looks like he's trying hard not to throw up, and a huge hug. "I'm so proud of you."

* * * *

I've never focused so hard on anything. I worked through the night, only taking a few minutes to catnap here and there. I've been drawing for so long that my hand is cramping and I think I might have done some permanent carpal tunnel damage. But I don't care. I'm afraid if I stop moving, I'm going to let the uncertainty creep back in. I can't let it. I'm going to get this design absolutely perfect and I'm going to win that damn competition if it kills me.

I tried to get Eddie to give me his opinion about which design I should submit but the man was so noncommittal. *They're both great. Whatever you think is better.* Urgh. I hate when people do that. So I kicked him out late last night. Besides, I don't need any distractions right now.

About hour twelve, I go cross-eyed after looking at my design for what feels like an eternity. I hate to admit it, but I need a break. I head down to the shop to steal a cup of coffee to recharge my batteries. The place is nearly empty, as usual in the post-morning rush. Jesús and Pops are in the back corner, arguing about the best movie of all time.

"I'm not saying Gene Kelly isn't adorable. A man that can dance is always sexy."

"And sing," Pops adds.

"Please, they all sing when they come to *Jesús*." He licks his finger and drags it down his chest making a sizzling sound.

Pops points to Jesús and tells me, "Such a modest young man. That's why I hired him."

"Look who's talking," I shoot back. It's the same debate they've been having for five years and neither will budge an inch. I slip behind the counter and start making my cappuccino.

"*Singin' in the Rain* is a good movie, but the *best* movie of all time? *Papi*, no," Jesús chides.

"Young Debbie Reynolds? How can you not love Debbie Reynolds? She was America's sweetheart," Pops counters with a finger wag.

"Debbie Reynolds is fabulous, but Robin Wright ain't no slouch. You can keep you singing, *Princess Bride* has princesses, sword fights and true love."

"Would you talk some sense into this kid?" Pops asks me, giving up and coming to stand by me on the other side of the counter.

"I'm not getting dragged into this. You both know my answer. *Psycho*. Hitchcock was a genius and romance is for suckers." There is a bitterness to my words that catches me by surprise. I guess I'm more annoyed at Eddie than I realized.

"How did I raise such a cynic?" Pops asks.

"Look, I'm not saying love doesn't exist. Of course it does." I skirt around the counter and take a small sip of my warm, frothy breakfast. "But people pretend that it's like a tattoo, this permanent mark you'll wear forever. Sure, you can see it that way, but the truth is it's only skin-deep. It may leave a mark, but you can always cut it out or cover it up."

They both stare at me with wide eyes and horrified expressions. Am I the only person left in the world who doesn't think love solves everything? I replay last night in my head, remembering how easy it was for Eddie to walk away.

"If you're not going to help, why don't you just leave?" I practically growled at Eddie. It was supposed to draw him out, to get him to rise to the challenge like he always has before. Instead, he just shut down.

"Is that what you want?" he asked with his hands in his pockets.

"Maybe, yeah. If you can't even be bothered to tell me which design is better." I crossed my arms and glared at him.

"I told you, I honestly think they're both amazing. Whatever you decide — "

"Enough!" I shouted at him and pointed to the door.

"You want to tell us why Eddie isn't around this morning?" Pops asks, drawing me out of my memories.

"I sent him home," I snap. "He was getting on my nerves."

"It's easy to fall in love with the idea of a man. It's a lot harder to live with them in reality," Jesús laments. He's a hopeless romantic, despite the *many* relationships that have proven exactly how hopeless it can be. "What did lover boy do this time?"

"He was being weird, treating me with kid gloves and being too nice."

"Even the best of us have our demons," Pops chimes in.

"Plus, I needed to focus."

"Here we go again." Jesús rolls his eyes.

"Excuse me?"

"Chica, you always do this. Obsess until you drive yourself—and the rest of us—completely *loca*. You know, you can try something without having to be absolutely perfect, right?"

"That's bullshit." I'm competitive, sure. But I'm not *obsessive*.

"Really? First your game which you lose countless hours of beauty sleep for. Then when that went to shit you jumped right in with Eddie. Now, you've kicked him out and it's all about this contest."

"It's not like that. This is important. Winning this contest is finally going to kickstart my graphic design career." *And make me finally feel like a legitimate artist.*

"Kiddo, I say this with nothing but love." Pops looks me square in the eye, places his hand on my forearm and squeezes. "Don't pin all your hopes to a single contest. Not everything good is popular and not everything popular is good. Love what you do and screw everyone else."

"So you don't think I can win?" My voice is high-pitched and sharp, giving away that I'm more hurt than angry.

"I didn't say that."

"He just means you're amazing, win or lose. You don't need a contest to prove that," Jesús adds.

"Are you two serious right now? Why is everyone always on me to do something with my life, then when I try, you all tell me I'm not good enough."

"That's not what we're saying."

"I don't need this. You know what, fuck you both. You're not invited to the launch party when E.B. Jericho unveils *my* new cover for her book."

I storm off back to my room. I pour every ounce of my frustration into my design. *I am going to win this if it kills me.*

Chapter Thirty

Eddie

Shit. Fuck. Goddamnit. Son of a bitch! My inner monologue has Tourette's.

"Eddie, you still there?" Benji asks on the other end of the line.

"Yeah, sorry. I'm here." *Just having a panic attack.* The earth is shifting under my feet, falling away until there's nothing keeping me from sinking down into the cold, dark, emptiness. "That's great news."

"Not like it's a surprise, we both knew Jackie's design was going to win. There were a lot of great entries this year, but hers was out of this world. Plus, the publisher loves the free publicity she's already getting us with that Instagram post from last week."

My stomach is a churning pit of anxiety and regret. Yes, Jackie's design is amazing. And yes, I knew she would win. I was so sure that I refused to help or give her any feedback—which she's still pissed about, despite the profuse apologizing I did the next morning to include surprise delivery from her favorite donut shop. I wanted this victory to be all hers. I even recused myself from the contest judging for the first time ever. That went over real well considering I refused to explain why.

The problem is she was so excited about the contest, finally having enough confidence in herself to go for it, I *still* haven't told her I'm E.B. Jericho. Which means there's still a ticking time bomb strapped to my heart. And knowing Jackie, my testicles.

"Let me give her the good news. I need to be the one to tell her," I sputter, knowing I'm signing my own death warrant.

* * * *

"I can't believe I'm finally going to see your place," Jackie hums at my side. She's been a lot less stressed after she submitted her final design to the contest. Things are still a bit awkward between us. We don't have the same easy banter and incessant teasing foreplay. But I feel like we're getting back to where we were before. That is, until I blow it all up tonight with my long-overdue confession.

She checks her email in the elevator up to my apartment, waiting for the results notification I know isn't coming. I take a deep breath and let it out slowly, willing myself to keep going. I owe her that much.

"I should've brought you here a long time ago," I lament. I squeeze her hand, trying to remember the way it feels in mine in case this is the last time she'll let me hold it.

"Had to take down all the Jonas Brothers posters?" she teases.

"I'm more of a Taylor Swift kind of guy," I deadpan, trying to keep the mood light despite the despair growing inside me. The elevator doors open, and I lead Jackie down the hallway to my front door. I take out my keys, but still before I can bring myself to unlock it. There's no getting out of it this time. As soon as she sees my place, she'll know.

I swallow hard, turn her to face me and tell her, "I just want you to know, I love you."

"I love you too, weirdo. Now stop freaking me out. You don't have a couch made out of people or anything do you?" She pokes me in the ribs.

"You don't know comfort until you've curled up in some soylent suede cushions."

She lets out a loud, raucous laugh. The beautiful sound nearly brings tears to my eyes. It is a sweet sucker-punch, adding to my guilt for being such a coward and dragging me deeper into my misery. *I am going to miss that sound.*

She tugs at my hand impatiently. "Come on already. You've seen my place. What are you so afraid of?"

Losing you.

With a resigned sigh, I place a soft kiss on her forehead, open the door and prepare to meet my fate.

Jackie lets go of my hand and strolls into my living room like a newly crowned queen surveying her realm. She takes in the high ceilings and open floor plan of my penthouse with an approving nod and a long, low whistle.

"Not bad, Khakis. Not bad at all. So, Fifty Shades of Beige, where's the sex dungeon?"

"No sex dungeon. Just a really big bed." I hover near the door, hands in my pockets, shuffling my feet and avoiding eye contact. I'm counting down the seconds I have left until the woman I love hates my guts.

"Guess that will have to do for now." She throws me a wink before scanning the rest of the room. I can tell the exact second my makeshift office catches her eye. She freezes in place, awe-struck, and lets out gasp and a low, "Whoa."

I like writing in an open space, so my desk is set up in a corner of my living room instead of one of the several spare bedrooms I rarely go into. The living room is twice as big as I need anyway and has the best views in the apartment. It's not like I throw parties here or anything, so it's never mattered that my work is on display.

Until now.

All the evidence she needs of the secret I've been keeping is staring her right in the face. I watch as she takes it all in. On the bookshelf are a handful of first edition copies of every one of my books, most have never been opened. On the desk are two finished manuscripts, including the one that will be published with her cover design. Above the desk, along the wall are poster-sized printings of my covers. On the end is the newest edition and my favorite, Jackie's design.

"And I thought I was a fan. Where did you get all this stuff?" she asks, drinking in each item before moving on to the next.

"Most of it is from my publisher." I try to keep my voice even and relaxed, despite the way my heart is thundering.

"Your publisher?" Jackie asks incredulously, not believing me.

I shrug and repeat myself. "My publisher." Waiting for her to realize the truth is a slow torture. Still, I can't bring myself to say the words that will end this. *Coward.* "The posters I had made and framed myself."

"Hey! That's mine." Jackie's eyebrows pinch together when she finally sees her artwork hanging on my wall. She strides over, standing in front of it with a wide, satisfied smile. "I thought you didn't care about my entry…"

"I care. More than you realize. I just wanted you to know you won all on your own." I come up behind her and place my hands on her hips. I try to remember the feel of her soft curves against my palms, saving the sensation with my most sacred memories. "Which you did. That is the winning entry in the E.B. Jericho cover design contest." I lean down and place a kiss on her shoulder and add, "Congratulations."

She spins to face me. Shock and excitement make her flush, her cheeks a beautiful shade of soft pink. "Oh my *God*! I won?"

"Yep." I smile wide at the joy splashed across her face.

"I won?" She starts to bounce on the tips of her toes, more excited than I've ever seen her. Her eyes are wide and watery. She is truly beautiful, down to her very soul.

"Yes," I tell her again. She wraps her arms around me and squeezes harder than I thought possible, squealing into my ear like a teapot about to boil over. I revel in the sheer happiness of this moment. All too quickly it slips through my fingers.

"Wait, how do you know I won?" She pulls back and studies me. I can see the wheels turning in her head, the realization dawning on her expression. Happiness giving way to confusion. Confusion to understanding. Understanding to sheer rage.

"Eddie, how do you know I won?" she asks, her words sharp as steel and aimed at my heart.

I clear my throat and step back. This is the moment. I need to be honest. I need to confess. But the words are stuck in the back of my throat. The further the silence stretches between us, the longer the lie continues, the angrier Jackie becomes.

"The posters. The books. All those hours typing away at your laptop. Making me guess what you do for a living! It was all some sick, twisted game to you," she snarls, prowling towards me. I take a step back for every forward lurch of hers, trying to keep a safe distance. "Say something!"

"It wasn't like that." I hold up my hands in defense, but I'm more terrified to lose her than I am scared of her.

"Oh really? Then why did you bring me here?"

I stare at my feet and run my fingers through my hair. My shoulders are slouched forward as if I'm carrying the sins of the world on my back. I open and close my mouth a dozen times, trying to find a way to say it. Words are usually my ally. My superpower. But today they have failed me. There are no words to explain to Jackie how sorry I am. How wrong I was. How deeply I love her.

"Tell me." Her eyes are ice, and her heart must have turned to stone. She isn't going to let me hide behind my cowardice any longer. "Say it, *goddammit*!" she screams at me.

"I'm...I'm E.B. Jericho," I finally manage to stammer.

For a moment, the world stops spinning. A suffocating stillness engulfs us, choking me with the urge to hold her. To sink to my knees and beg forgiveness when all I can do is stand and stare. Then everything happens lurches forward at light speed as if to catch up.

"You *asshole*. You gaping, prolapsed *anus*. You lying, manipulative, conniving piece of shit," Jackie shouts at me, at the ceiling, at the world itself. She is pacing back and forth in front of my desk. The rapid rise and fall of her chest tells me she is breathing hard, whether that's from the pacing or anger I'm not sure.

She grabs the first thing she can get her hands on, a copy of *Honourbound*, the book she was reading when we met. I'd be amused by the irony if I weren't too busy being equally heartbroken and terrified. She winds up and launches it at my head. Luckily, books have horrible aerodynamics, and I have decent reflexes. The book goes sailing past me and into my kitchen. Undeterred, she continues her assault until she clears a shelf and has run through her entire extensive repertoire of swear words.

Exhausted but still angry, she stands stalk still and peers right through me. "How could you?" The betrayal in her voice crushes me.

"Jackie, I'm so sorry. I didn't mean—"

"Giving me that sketch pad. Pushing me to enter the contest. That *damn* Instagram post. Winning the contest. It was all you?" She is connecting dots that aren't related and drawing the worst possible picture of my intentions. She doesn't give me time to answer. To explain.

"No—"

"You made me think I could…" She lets out a long, low growl. "God, how could I be so stupid?" She slams her palm against her temple three times, hard enough to leave an angry red blotch.

"You're brilliant," I tell her, reaching out to grab her wrist.

"Fuck you!" she snaps and pulls away. "You manipulated me into playing your games. Entering your stupid contest. Caring about you. And for what? To trick me into getting my shit together? To mold me into the woman you want me to be?"

Sadness and betrayal overtake her anger, and I want to throw myself off the tallest cliff I can find for hurting her. For making her doubt herself when all I ever wanted was for her to see what she is capable of.

"No, that's not it at all. I don't want you to be anything except what you are right now. Okay, maybe a little less rabid, but…" I try to lighten the mood with humor and immediately regret it. That was the absolute wrong answer.

"Rabid?" she seethes. I wince at the word.

An unsettling calmness overtakes her. She stands up straight, her hands falling to her sides. Her face is wiped blank. *I'm about to die.* She meanders over to the framed poster of her design hanging on my wall, rips it down and smashes it against the corner of my desk. Glass shatters across my floor like the broken shards of our relationship.

Jackie tosses the frame aside like so much trash. She locks eyes with me, and I freeze in place, like prey too afraid to pick a direction to run. With her head held high and her shoulders back, she struts up to me with an easy confidence. She steps into me until our chests are nearly touching. She is close enough I can smell the caramel scent on her skin.

With a simper and a sweet timbre she tells me, "You come anywhere near this rabid bitch again, and I'll rip your throat out."

Jackie turns and walks out of my apartment—out of my life— without so much as a backward glance.

Chapter Thirty-One

Jackie

When I left Eddie's apartment, I thought I would be angry for the rest of my life. I thought he'd managed to flip some switch in my brain where I could only see red. Rage and hate would color my days until the end of time. But, by the time I got home, I was too exhausted to be angry. I was too exhausted to think. I fell into bed and wrapped myself up in the darkest despair I've ever experienced. All I can do is stare at my ceiling, cry and sleep.

I'm sick. Sick and tired of being sad. Of feeling hurt. Of being lost. I've hardly left my bed, much less my apartment, for well over a week. Thank god for delivery drivers or I would've starved to death by now.

Everyone has tried to cheer me up. To get me out of here. Elizabeth tempted me with a trip out to see her and Man Meat. I declined. Jesús offered to take me salsa dancing and play wingman. I refused. Pops even tried to bribe me with promises of rainbow sherbet with rainbow unicorn sprinkles. I almost cracked at that one. I may be a strong, independent woman, but who doesn't love rainbow sprinkles? In the end I told him to bring it to me in bed or fuck off.

What's the point of any of it? At the end of the day, I'm still going to crawl back into bed, the same old me with the same old inadequacies.

A firm rat-a-tat-tat on my door has me already annoyed.

"What now?" I holler, not bothering to get out of bed.

To my unending surprise, in walks my mom, put-together as always and wearing even more disappointment in her features than usual. *Pops has got to be desperate if he called Mom.*

"I see the extra time you've spent at home hasn't resulted in any cleaning frenzies." She picks up a dirty pair of pajama pants off the floor, revealing a Chinese food carton underneath. *That's what happened to the rest of my spring rolls.* The look of disgusted horror on my mom's face brings the first smile to my lips in days. She uses the pajamas as makeshift gloves to throw out the carton before tossing them in my laundry hamper. Then she turns her laser focus on me.

"I don't have the energy to do this with you, Mom." I plead for her to just let me be for once. I grab my blanket and throw it over my head like I used to do when I was eight and didn't want to go to school.

"Too bad. Your grandfather may be content to let you waste away in here until the smell reaches high heaven, but I am not. Come on. Get up." She rips the blanket off with shocking strength. "I did not raise a quitter."

"No, just a failure," I deadpan, staring up at the ceiling and still refusing to move.

"What are you on about?"

"I failed, okay. At college. At being a graphic designer. At being in a relationship. At being a daughter. At being a fucking adult. At everything I've ever tried. I'm a failure. Are you happy now?"

I cross my arms and pout. My mom sighs and shakes her head.

"You are always so melodramatic. You get that from your grandfather." She shoves me over and sits down on the bed next to me. "You only fail if you stop trying."

This woman is like a walking, talking motivational poster. I should stick her on the wall next to my *hang in there* kitten picture.

She pokes me in the ribs with her long, manicured fingernail, a move she must've learned from Pops. "And you'd have to start trying before you could stop."

"What's that supposed to mean?" I ask, exasperated. I sit up and study her, wondering for a minute how the apple could fall so far from the tree. *Maybe I was switched at birth.*

"It means you've never put your whole heart, your whole self, into a single thing you do. You could be anything. Achieve anything, if only you would get out of your own way," Mom answers matter-of-factly.

I reel at the backhanded compliment. My mom actually believes in me. *Sort of.*

"And your grandfather isn't doing you any favors by letting you tread water," she adds with her familiar judgmental lilt.

"Tread water? He throws me a life ring, and you'd rather I drown." I shake my head and toss myself back on the mattress.

"No, Jacqueline. I'm begging you to swim to shore."

The analogy hits home. I feel adrift, floating wherever the current takes me, too afraid to choose the wrong direction. A shore I'll never reach.

Just when my mom almost has me believing she has a point, she goes and adds, "Besides, I don't see how what Eddie did was so very horrible. So he lied about what he does. Plenty of men do that. I once dated a mailroom clerk who told me he was the head of distribution for a major corporation. He left out the mail part entirely."

I put my pillow over my face and scream. Leave it to my mother to trivialize my suffering.

"You don't get it. It's not just the lie," I try to explain. "The lie is the tree that bore the poison fruit. The whole relationship was a lie. He made me believe I was good at something. Then his lie took that away. I didn't just lose him. I lost who I thought I could be."

"Don't be stupid. He didn't take anything away."

"Excuse you." *Is it wrong to want to wring my mother's neck? Yes. Do I daydream about doing it anyway? Also yes.*

"People can't take away who you are. You will always be every bit the amazing, stubborn, talented, infuriating woman you've ever been. Believe me. Trying to get you to be anything other than who you are is a lost cause. I've always envied that about you."

"And hated it in Pops," I quip without missing a beat. I can't stand her revisionist history.

"That's different. Finding himself was more important than being my father."

"You were in your thirties."

"And I'm not ashamed to admit I still needed my father," she snips, her tone defensive and irritated. She takes a quiet moment to herself, I'm sure compartmentalizing her emotions in the detached way she does. But when she speaks again, there's an unfamiliar wistfulness to her voice. "You never stop being a parent. Or wanting what's best for your child, even when they're an adult."

Staring down at me, still defiantly prone on the bed, she tucks a strand of hair behind my ear and cups my face. It's a sweet, gentle gesture that makes me feel five years old again. Back when we were still a family — before Dad left, and I started disappointing her.

"You know I love you, don't you?" she asks. I nod, but don't meet her eyes.

"Sometimes I just wish you liked me more," I confess.

"I'm sorry you feel that way. I just don't know how to talk to you sometimes." She lets out a sad sigh. "I wish you liked me too."

I risk glancing over at my mother, sitting on the edge of my unmade bed and lamenting our strained relationship. For the first time, I let myself realize she really is trying. I have never made it easy for her, but she keeps coming back. She keeps trying. God knows we are two *very* different people, but Pops was right. She loves me and she wants what's best for me. Even if she's going about it back-ass-wards in a way that makes me want to scream bloody murder. I climb out of my own pit of wallowing long enough to throw the woman who carried me for nine months a bone.

I sit up and tell her, "You know I love you too, right?"

She cracks a small smile and pats my hand. "I know. We are just two very different people. And that's okay." She sounds like she's trying to convince herself more than me. She picks up my hand, still stained with ink and the nails gnawed down to the quick. "You know you intimidate me?"

"What?" I balk. *That can't be true.*

"You're full of so much raw talent. You always have been. I never knew how to help you harness it. I know I push you too hard sometimes. I meant to push you forward and I think I just pushed you away. And I'm sorry. I just don't know how else to help you."

My mom holds my hand, and we both stare at it like we're Alice peering through the looking glass. Her honesty shocks and humbles me.

"You know you inspire me?" I tell her.

"What?" She has the same stunned reaction I did a few minutes ago, and I smile at the familiarity in her features.

"You do. Your ability to just keep going." I swallow the lump in my throat and broach the subject we silently agreed never to talk about. "Dad left us. He took off, and I was so scared and hurt, I shut out the world. But you just kept going. You rolled up your sleeves and kept living."

"Oh, Jackie," Mom exclaims before wrapping me in a big hug. She rocks us back and forth ever so softly, humming in my ear.

"How do you do it? How do you push through the fear?" I ask my mom with my face buried against her silk blouse. She strokes my back, and I sink into the welcome comfort.

"Your grandmother used to say, life keeps on going, whether you're living it or not."

I chuckle. "Pops uses that line all the time."

"Well, I guess I decided to keep living. Nothing plus a little effort might still be nothing, but it might also be everything."

"It's that simple, huh?" I let my snark bubble up to the surface.

"That hard," she answers, kissing the top of my head. We sit in the silence, embracing and soaking in the knowledge that as different as we are, we love each other. And right now, that is enough.

"You're wrong about one thing," I mumble, not entirely sure I want to be heard.

"What's that?"

"With Eddie, I did try. With my whole heart." I let the tears fall. They aren't the overwhelming sobs of lost hope I've shed over the past week. They are the gentle acceptance of moving on.

"Then I'm truly sorry." She squeezes me tighter, and I surrender to the sentimentality of it all.

Mom lets me enjoy the tender moment for a few more minutes before her cursed indomitable spirit kicks into overdrive. She never was one to sit still for long. She pulls away and stands up with a quick couple claps of her hands.

"Chop. Chop. Life keeps on going, so you better start living it. And there's no time like the present." Her cheery voice rings through the apartment. She's back to the overbearing woman I am trying to learn to appreciate. "Let's start with getting this place habitable again. Starting with changing these rancid sheets."

With a reluctant groan, I roll out of bed and get to work.

Chapter Thirty-Two

Eddie

"She was *explicitly* clear she does *not* want to see you," Darla tells me while blocking my exit from her office with her superhero stance. In her case, maybe it is an evil-villain stance. She is literally the last thing standing between me and the woman I love.

Knowing Jackie is in the building, within a few hundred feet of where I'm standing, is killing me. I haven't seen her in weeks and I'm going mad. She won't answer my phone calls or emails. And every time I've tried going to her place, Pops and Jesús run interference, not even letting me in the front door of the shop.

"I just need five minutes," I plead.

"She is here to sign the contract for her cover design and that's it. This isn't going to be some cheesy love story moment where she comes running back to your open arms. Pull your head out of your ass." Darla has been pretty vocal about how badly she thinks I screwed up.

With Jackie and with my career.

The publisher is pissed. I finally finished the manuscript for *Glory's End*, the last book in the *Sins of Tomorrow* series, but we're behind schedule. We had to push the entire production process back a month. Luckily, we'll still make the publication date, but there's less time for publicity now. They tried to force me into a few public appearances to make up for it. One executive even had the audacity to suggest we use my relationship with Jackie as a hook. Star-crossed lovers brought together by a passion for words. *A hook.* I channeled my inner Jackie and told them to fuck right the hell off. I'd rather be sued for breach of contract.

Not that any of that matters to me now. It's hard to care about much of anything when the woman I love hates me more than anything on this earth.

If only I could get two minutes to talk to her. To explain and apologize. There has to be a way to make this better.

But first I have to get past Darla.

"This is ridiculous. You're my agent, not my jailer."

"Right now, I'm both. I spent weeks fixing the mess you made. You aren't going to so much as breathe on that woman." Her voice is flat, and her gaze is focused. She's not going to willingly let me talk to Jackie.

"Fine. I give up." I flop down on the couch in the corner, deflated and defeated.

Darla isn't buying it. She keeps her post in front of the door, her watchful eyes trained on me. I throw my arm over my face and pretend to wallow. It takes about fifteen minutes before Darla lets herself get distracted by her ever-pinging phone. Another fifteen before she moves away from the door. Still, the second I stand, she is laser focused on me again.

"Where exactly do you think you're going?" She leans forward on her desk, imposing and menacing.

"To the bathroom." I take three large steps toward the door.

"Hold it," Darla tells me, stepping around her desk and in front of me.

"Darla, I'm a grown man. I'm not going to be told when I can use the restroom." She doesn't budge. I roll my eyes and sigh. "I get it, all right? This isn't the time or the place. I'm not going to do anything stupid." The lie rolls off my tongue, and I'd feel guilty if I weren't doing it to get to Jackie.

"Fine. To the men's room and right back. And I swear, you cause any more drama and I will make you regret it."

I give her a mock salute and click my heels together. "Yes, boss."

She opens the door to her office, and I make a beeline for the conference room. *Sorry, Darla.*

When I first catch a glimpse of Jackie standing behind the glass wall of the conference room, the sight knocks the wind out of me. She has somehow managed to become more beautiful over the past few weeks.

Her fiery red hair is now the deep indigo of the sea during a storm. Curling in soft waves over her shoulders, it turns light turquoise at the tips like the sky on a clear summer day. My fingers itch to run through the silky strands. She's wearing a cropped leather jacket and skin-tight black leggings that have all her amazing curves on display. My body aches with how much I've missed her. Underneath the jacket, I can just make out the writing on her black T-shirt. *I run a tight shipwreck.* I smirk at the very Jackie saying.

She makes her way to the door, along with the handful of other people in the room. I can't be bothered to figure out who else is with her. Drinking in the sight of Jackie takes all my attention. Someone holds the conference room door open, and she steps through it. Now there is nothing between me and the woman I love except her resentment and my regret.

"Hello, Jackie." My voice is shaky with nerves.

She stops dead in her tracks and stares at me. The whole office goes silent, or maybe I just can't hear it over the drumming of blood in my ears. She looks me over, from toes to the tip of my head. It reminds me of the first time we met. Being again subjected to her scrutiny makes my palms sweat.

"Hello, Edwin," she answers, her voice dry and devoid of emotion. I didn't think she'd call me Khakis but using my full name stings with detached impersonality. I'd prefer she called me asshole or dickhead or anything that showed she still felt something for me, even anger. "I was wondering if you'd have the balls to crash the party."

"You have some nerve." A woman's voice draws my attention away from Jackie for the first time, and I'm surprised to see her mom standing next to her.

"Ms. Ryan," I greet her. "Nice to see you again."

"Go to hell," she retorts. Jackie cracks a small smile at her mom's answer.

"Already there, Ms. Ryan," I admit. Catching Jackie's gaze, I stare into her eyes and silently plead for a second chance.

"We are leaving." Jackie brushes past me with a frigid indifference.

"Jackie, can we talk?" I ask, following after her like a lost puppy.

"No." She doesn't bother stopping or even looking at me when she says it.

"Eddie!" Darla shouts from across the office like the needle scratching across a vinyl record.

Panic wells up inside me as the chance to make things right begins slipping through my fingers. I'm not going to have another chance. In sheer desperation, I grab Jackie's wrist and turn her to face me as the words come pouring out.

"Jackie, I'm sorry. I swear to you, I didn't mean for it to go this far. But how was I supposed to tell you?"

She rips her wrist out of my hand like the touch was searing her skin. "A million different ways a million different times, you fucking coward!" she screams in my face.

Oddly enough, her anger fills me with hope. If she's angry, she still cares. I keep going, ignoring Darla at my back telling me to walk away.

"You're right. I'm a coward. I was afraid of losing you. But can you blame me? Every time I got close, you'd find some asinine reason to push me away. I couldn't hand you the excuse to run on a golden platter."

"Don't you dare turn this back around on me. I'm not the lying, manipulative, backstabbing coward."

We are full-on shouting at each other in front of the entire office and neither one of us gives a goddamn. In my peripheral vision, I sense Darla and Ms. Ryan hatching a plan to separate us. It may involve a fire hose.

"You act like it was so easy. Like I could casually tell you I was this person you'd idolized, that you'd built up to be someone completely different in your head."

"And you think it's easy to forget that you are a conniving asshole? Forget that you made a fool out of me and thank my lucky stars that you deigned to be with me?"

"No. Of course not. But, maybe you should admit you'd never have been brave enough to share your work without my push. I shoved you out of the rut you'd dug yourself into." I'll admit, part of me is angry at her too. For pretending like it all meant nothing. For being able to walk away.

"Oh, that's rich coming from you, *E.B. Jericho*."

"What's that supposed to mean?"

"It means you're not just a liar, you're a hypocrite." She steps into my space, close enough I could reach out and touch her if I were a braver man. She doesn't bother to lower her voice despite the proximity. "You write these amazing books, but you're too much of a pussy to put your own name on them! If you're so brave, why don't you stand up and tell the world E.B. Jericho is really an obnoxious, uptight, self-righteous jackass."

"That's completely different." But for the life of me I can't think why. "Lots of authors have pen names."

"Bullshit," she challenges.

She's snarling with her eyes wide and wild. I can't read her mind, but I'd bet the image of murdering me in some outlandish way is playing in her head right now. I keep pushing. I can't help myself. If she's arguing with me at least she's still talking to me. Maybe there's still hope.

"At least I'm still putting my work out there. How many notebooks full of sketches do you have squirrelled away in your apartment where no one will ever see them? How many times have you been too scared to take a chance on yourself? How many years have you wasted slinging coffee because you're so afraid to fail you don't bother to try?"

She recoils like I slapped her. Her mouth snaps shut, and she pinches her eyebrows together and stares at me with a tortured wonder. Knowing I'm right doesn't change how much I regret saying those words out loud.

A collective gasp fills the sudden silence of the busy office. The crowd I hadn't noticed building around us starts to dissipate with no one willing to make eye contact with me.

"Eddie, you've said quite enough." Darla places a hand on my forearm and pulls me back.

Ms. Ryan leans in and whispers something to Jackie I can't hear. She gives a subtle shake of her head in response and waves her off. Jackie turns away from me and presses the elevator button without a word.

I twist out of Darla's grasp and turn back to Jackie. The quiet rage of her locked jaw juxtaposed to the clear devastation in her watery eyes makes me want to claw my own skin off. I did that to her and it's killing me.

I have to fix this. There has to be a way to fix this.

"I'm sorry. I shouldn't have said any of that. You're right. I'm a liar and a coward. I was scared to lose you, so I lied to you. I did it over and over again until I didn't know how to stop. And I live with that regret every day. But this can't be it. This *can't* be the end." She's staring straight forward, focused on the elevator doors with singular intensity. "Jackie, I love you. And I'm so sorry. Just tell me, what can I do to make this right?"

The elevator dings and Jackie steps into it with her mom at her side. She finally meets my gaze. Her eyes are cold as death and cut me to my core. I've lost her. I can feel it deep in my bones.

"You can go fuck yourself," Jackie tells me as the doors close.

* * * *

"On a scale from one to ten, how bad did I mess that up?" I ask Darla back in her office that I now regret ever leaving.

"You turned your asshatery up to eleven, my friend," she answers.

"Oh Jesus," I whine, burying my head in my hands. "I just made it so much worse, didn't I?"

Darla places a hand on my shoulder and gives me the brutal honesty I expect from her. "Yes. You did."

"You were right, okay?" I shoot out of my chair. "I'm sorry. I promise, next time I will listen to you."

"No, you won't." She sighs, knowing me well enough to know better.

"You're right. I probably won't, but I need you right now. I need your help to fix this."

"Eddie, honestly, I don't think there is a way to fix this. That woman seems pretty sure she's done with you."

"I have a plan." I stand up, place my palms flat on her desk and lean in. "How fast could you get something new published?"

"Look," she starts as she steeples her hands on her desk. I'm definitely getting the *it's-not-me-it's-you* talk. "A new Jericho series isn't the answer."

"I wrote her something," I blurt out.

Darla cracks a smile, catching on to what I'm getting at.

"You sneaky son of a bitch. Is that what you've been working on instead of making your contract deadlines?" I nod and she shakes her head. "What are you pitching?"

"I guess you'd call it...a love letter."

Darla's shrewd eyes study me. "Is it any good?"

"Benji says it's the best thing I've ever written."

"It's worth a shot, I guess. I'll call the publisher. I'm sure any new Jericho book will probably get an automatic green light, even if it is completely different."

"No. This isn't a Jericho book. I want—no, I *need*—to publish this one as myself. As Edwin Jaworski. No pen names. No hiding."

"That's a hard one. Pitching a book of an unknown author is never easy."

"And I want to publish it as soon as possible. Next month." I lay it out there, throwing the gauntlet at Darla's feet and knowing she'll thrive on the challenge.

"Eddie, that's not going to happen." Darla shakes her head in violent disbelief.

"I need this, Darla. Please. Find me a publisher and get it released next month, and I'll give you thirty percent of the royalties."

"Goddamn it," she says with a resigned acceptance. "Fine. You're lucky I'm a hopeless romantic."

I leave Darla to the million phone calls she needs to make and make a silent wish she can work magic.

Chapter Thirty-Three

Jackie

"That's suicide." Elizabeth's concern only serves to convince me.

"Ye of little faith. Besides, what does it matter? The game is ending in a few months anyway," I tell my best friend. I've decided to end in a blaze of glory. Woman'sWorld will not fade into the night. "I'm going down swinging."

"Jackie, think this through," Elizabeth pleads. She's far too rational to change my mind. I'm following my gut. "You could lose everything."

I already have.

"Fuck it," I answer as I brazenly pick a fight with the strongest alliance in Rule Them All. Their forces outnumber mine ten-to-one. Elizabeth is right. It's suicide, and I don't care. I'm in the mood to burn it all to the ground.

Rule Them All is ending. Eddie is gone. And my career as a graphic designer is over before it started now that I've withdrawn my cover design from the competition. I'm trying to hit rock bottom so hard I bounce.

"I'm sorry, Jackie. I love you, but I can't watch this," Elizabeth tells me. Her forlorn voice only shakes my confidence for a second.

She signs off, and I trudge forward.

It takes five hours to destroy what I spent nearly a decade building. I fight to the last man, woman and child. I tear down my country until there is nothing left. Vanquished and broken, I crawl into bed after two in the morning.

I've never felt so hollow.

An untold number of hours later, I'm startled out of my restless slumber by a determined thumping on my door. I check my phone and confirm it's Wednesday, my day off. Whoever it is can fuck off indefinitely.

"Go away!" I shout at the unknown interloper to my wallowing.

The pounding gets louder. Three confident *thwacks*, a five second pause, then three more *thwacks*.

"I said, go away." I groan and pull the bed sheets up over my head, but the persistent knocking just keeps coming. I stomp over to the door and fling it open with an angry, "What?"

"Oh good, you're awake," a slender woman in classy business attire says with a sarcastic lilt. She steps around me and into the apartment before I can slam the door in her face. "I'm Darla Sinclair with the Moirai Literary Agency."

"You're here about the cover design." I slam the door closed and cross my arms. I know Eddie's publisher is pissed about me pulling out, but I haven't heard anything for the past few days. I thought they'd finally given up. Apparently not if they're sending executive henchmen — or women — to pressure me into it. Too bad for her I refuse to be intimidated.

"Yes. I'm here about the cover design." She sets down her briefcase and takes off her expensive-looking wool coat, folding it neatly and draping it over the briefcase. My blatant animosity doesn't seem to register as she wanders around my tiny apartment, taking in my newly barren walls and empty bookshelf. I got rid of all my copies of his books and tore down all the old sketches hanging on my walls. There is a visible hole where Eddie — and E.B. Jericho — used to be.

"I've already told you guys I'm not—"

"I'm aware of what you've told the publisher," she cuts me off with calm efficiency. "I'm not here on their behalf, but rather on yours. I'm here because you're being a complete fucking idiot."

My mouth drops open, and I stare at her in surprise. Between being half asleep and now completely stunned, I've lost my power of speech.

"Do you realize you're giving up the opportunity of a lifetime?" she continues.

"I don't need the sales pitch. It's not happening." I snap back into the fight. "Sorry, but you're going to have to find some other sucker."

"Again, I'm not with the publisher. And despite owning the copyright to your work as part of the entry agreement for the contest, they have already found another artist. Eddie, consummate pain in my ass that he is, used his contractually required cover approval to insist they not use your design without your consent. A sweet, but misguided gesture on his part."

I ignore the revelation that Eddie stood up for me — it's the least he could do after everything — and focus on the realization that I've met her before. And that she's a friend of Eddie's.

"That's where I recognize you from!" I point at her, anger boiling over in my veins. "You're Eddie's lackey."

"I assure you, I am no one's lackey. And I am most definitely *not* here on Eddie's behalf."

"Oh, yeah? Then what the hell do you care?"

She pulls out the chair from my desk and sits down. Crossing her legs and folding her hands in her lap, she takes a deep sigh, as if recharging her patience.

"I care that a strong and talented woman is throwing away an amazing opportunity to spite a man." She sounds disgusted and disappointed.

"Bullshit," I retort, but her conviction has me wavering. "You can leave now and take your presumptuous opinions with you."

"Explain to me why you refuse to seize an opportunity that you've earned, and I will leave."

Darla sits there, studying me with her cool eyes. I have three choices. I can answer her question, try to drag her out of my apartment or embrace my new roommate because she is clearly not going anywhere otherwise.

"I don't like being lied to and manipulated. And nepotism isn't my deal. I don't need Eddie's handouts to be successful."

"How is winning a contest a handout?" Her voice is even despite the condescension.

"When your boyfriend is the judge, it isn't much of a contest, is it?"

"Eddie recused himself."

"He what?" I stutter.

"He flat-out refused to vote, or even provide any direction as to what he wanted for the cover. It actually caused quite a shitstorm for me, so thanks for that."

I'm reeling from this new information. I assumed Eddie was the only reason I won. The only reason I *could've* won. If that's not true, I'm not sure where I stand. I take a few moments to replay the past few months, rethinking why I even entered.

"He still posted that picture on Instagram. That had to have influenced the contest," I argue, trying to maintain the moral high ground. "He didn't have to actually vote to rig it."

"If you buy a book after a friend recommends it, was it your choice or were you manipulated?" Darla's response comes quicker than I can effectively counter.

"That's different."

"It's not," she declares. "I've been trying for years to get Eddie to interact more with his audience despite his stubborn refusals and privacy complaints. Your mural is exactly the type of content his publicist should've been hunting for. Which I informed them of when I threatened to fire them if they don't drastically improve his social media engagement. That post is his most popular all year and resulted in a five percent increase in *Sins of Tomorrow* sales across two weeks. I have no doubt it has done more for his career than yours."

I take a moment to absorb her words. I don't want to admit it, but I know she is right. I've followed E.B. Jericho's social media for years and nothing has ever gotten this much buzz other than release announcements. Still, my nagging insecurity won't let me accept her justification.

"He still pushed me into the contest."

"Did he design your entry?"

"Of course not." I recoil from the accusation. "But I've been wanting to enter for years. I wouldn't have done it this year without him." I'm embarrassed by the admission, but it's true. Between Eddie's daily support and the shot of confidence from his Instagram post, this year was different. It's not that I *couldn't* have done it without him — it's just that I know I *wouldn't* have. He was right. I was comfortable in my rut.

"So what? It's still your work." Darla shrugs. "I keep Eddie focused and on task. Every book he's published has been with me riding him to meet deadlines. Does that make it any less his work? His success?"

"That's your job," I remind her.

"Isn't being supportive the job of any real partner? If Eddie weren't E.B. Jericho, would it matter that he encouraged you?" she counters.

"Maybe not, but it still feels wrong. I didn't earn it," I tell her honestly.

"Yes, you did. You just don't think you *deserve* it." Her words are flat and matter-of-fact, like she's speaking a truth beyond argument. *Maybe she is.*

"The only thing stopping you from being successful is you." Darla stands, puts on her coat and picks up her briefcase. She pulls out a cream business card with gold embossed lettering and sets it on my desk. "If you get over your imposter syndrome, give me a call."

Darla strolls to the door, opening it for herself while I stand around in stunned silence. I feel naked. *Exposed.*

"You can tell Eddie this doesn't change anything." I lash out, desperately trying to question her motives and undermine her words. "I don't care if I'm drowning in graphic design work, I'm not going to forgive him."

"Eddie doesn't know I'm here and, as far as I'm concerned, he never needs to. I don't care if you ever speak to him again." Darla has a devious smile curling her thin lips, but I'm not sure I believe her. "I hope to hear from you, Jaqueline."

I stumble back to bed and collapse on the covers. My mind is a churning mess of what-ifs and maybes.

What if I won the competition purely on merit?

Maybe I should keep the cover design offer.

What if I could make it as a graphic designer?

Maybe I should call Darla.

One thing I don't question—I know I still don't forgive Eddie.

Chapter Thirty-Four

Jackie

"If you say one word, I'll cut your balls off and hang them from my rearview mirror like fuzzy dice," I shout at Eddie from across Beans & Dreams while brandishing a plastic knife so he knows I'm serious.

It pisses me off that he has the belligerent audacity to show up here after the shit he's pulled. I'm instantly livid at the sight of him. My heart is racing, and my mouth is dry. It is rage bubbling inside me, not an insatiable longing to be wrapped up in Eddie's arms. To have him whisper that he loves me and actually be able to forgive him. *Nope. Definitely just rage.* I hate Edwin Jaworski.

Eddie stops just inside the door. Our eyes lock, and my chest tightens. It's been months since the blow-ups in his apartment and at his office. I thought I was moving on. I'm swamped with graphic design work, as Darla promised I would be. I'm crazy busy and barely have time to think about Eddie. I hardly miss his lips and his hands. His words and his cuddles. The way his warm body felt wrapped around mine in bed. I thought I was forgetting him, but I thought wrong.

I force a scowl and glare at him. We're alone in the shop, and I can't help but wonder if he intended it to be that way. I'm only working a few hours these days, filling in when needed really. Has he been watching and waiting to be able to catch me alone? *No witnesses to the crime.* That's brave.

To my surprise, he doesn't move closer. He doesn't say a word. Instead, with one hand he pinches his lips shut. I remember doing the same thing to him the first day we met. The tiniest bit of my resentment melts at the sight. He must be able to tell because a small smile curls his pinched lips. I shake off the tenderness welling up inside of me and resume my death stare. If looks could kill, he'd be a dead man.

With his free hand he unclips his messenger bag and blindly riffles through it. He pulls out a small book, holds it to his chest over his heart, lets out a long breath through his nose and sets it on the table next to him. Then he leaves. He just walks away. I can't believe it.

I run to the door, throwing it wide open but he's already disappeared like a figment of my imagination. I'd doubt he was ever here at all if it weren't for the small book still sitting on the table. The cover is all black with simple white lettering that reads,

Hurts
A Lot Like
Love
By Edwin B. Jaworski

"Holy fuck," I mutter. He did it. The crazy son of a bitch actually published a book under his own name. Part of me is desperate to run upstairs, lock the door and devour Eddie's words. But the stronger, more stubborn part of me refuses to give him the satisfaction. I leave the book on the table, forgotten and unnoticed.

The minutes tick by, and I avoid looking at the unwelcome addition to the coffee shop. I wander around the room, wiping down tables and straightening chairs. When I get to the table with Eddie's book on it, I'm pissed at myself for leaving it there. For letting it sit on the front table like it deserves a place of honor. It doesn't deserve to exist at all. Not in my world, and certainly not in my coffee shop. I pick up the offensive literature and open it in the middle, determined to tear it in two.

My hands still mid-air. *You're being ridiculous. Books aren't evil.* I chide myself for being so petty. I hate it when someone dog-ears a page and I was ready to rip this innocent book apart. *Shame on me.*

Still, I can't leave it sitting out. The sight of it will drive me nuts all day. I stick it in my apron pocket and promptly forget about it. *Yeah, right.*

Climbing up the stairs to my apartment, the stiff book in my pocket is an ever-present reminder of the hole in my life where Eddie used to be. I pull the book out and toss it on the near-empty bookshelf. A slip of paper slides out from between the pages and curiosity gets the better of me.

I walk up to the book cautiously, as if it were a living, feral thing that could attack at any moment. In all honesty, I don't feel entirely safe with it in my home. I fell in love with Eddie's words before I ever met him. They are more dangerous to me than anything else in this world. But I refuse to be intimidated by a man who isn't even here.

I pick up the book with an irreverent swipe of my hand and crack it open to the page near the beginning where the paper is sticking out. I purposefully stretch the binding of the new book, getting a sick pleasure in hearing the virgin spine crack under the pressure.

It is a flyer, simple black and white like the book cover, for a book signing. It is at the small coffee shop down the street a week from today. I know it is his way of inviting me to talk. I shake my head and hold back a laugh. If someone told me a year ago that E.B. Jericho was going to be doing a book signing less than a mile away, I would've lost my shit. Now? I'd rather throw myself into a vat of acid than go anywhere near that bookstore.

"Nice try," I tell the small flyer before crumpling it up and throwing it in the trash at my feet.

Before I'm able to close the book, I notice it's open to the dedication page. My brain starts reading the words as if by reflex. I can't stop myself.

Dedication
For Ignis.
An awe-inspiring artist.
A poet with profanity.
A god-awful barista.
And the irrefutable love of my life.

I slap the cover closed and throw the book across the room like it's a ticking bomb. My heart is in my throat, and I'm breathing heavier than if I'd tried to deadlift a grand piano. My mind is racing, and my stomach is churning. I pace around the room muttering and groaning to myself. *Why did I have to pick it up? I should've shoved it down the garbage disposal!*

I hate Eddie for writing those words, but I hate myself more for how desperately I want to read them. *Is this how drug addicts feel?* The book lies in the corner of the room, like a coiled snake waiting to strike. It's out of sight but never out of my mind. Two long, painful hours drag on where my willpower slowly erodes.

He'll never know if you read it. No one will ever have to know. I reason with myself, rationalizing the mistake I know I'm inevitably going to make.

"Fuck it," I finally groan before swiping up the book, lying down in my bed and devouring Eddie's words like a glutton twelve hours into a diet—with shameful reckless abandon.

It is three in the morning when I put the book down. I have read it cover to cover three times, cried over it six times, laughed out loud eight and picked up the phone to call Eddie a dozen or more before tossing it aside in conflicted frustration.

The next few days are a blur. I'm a zombie functioning on little sleep and a brain so scrambled I don't know which way is up. I make the catastrophic mistake of leaving Eddie's book on the counter one morning and now both Jesús and Pops have read his confession/apology to me.

"I fell for Ignis faster than a fat kid on a seesaw," Jesús stands on a chair and bellows out to the patrons of Beans & Dreams as soon as I step through the door. The disgusting hopeless romantic has taken to dramatic recitation of his favorite passages any time I show my face. *As if I didn't have the damn book memorized by now!* He keeps a copy of *Hurts A Lot Like Love* under the counter with his favorite sections highlighted for quick reference. It's a bizarre form of hell I find myself trapped in.

"'It wasn't her stunning beauty — although I could stare into her eyes for an eternity — or her arresting wit, although I would be lucky to quarrel with her until the day I die. It was, quite unironically, her heart that captured mine. She hid the delicate artifact under the cover of disinterestedness and behind the barbed wired of sarcastic hostility, but deep down, Ignis was a gooey marshmallow.'"

"Better sleep with one eye open because this marshmallow is going to murder you in your sleep, JC!" I threaten him for the millionth time, knowing it will do me no good.

The five customers we have give him a subdued round of applause. I beeline it for the cappuccino maker to get my morning fix and get out of Dodge. JC isn't going to let me get away that easy. He sidles up next to me with an obnoxious grin. The book clutched to his chest, he gives me googly eyes like a fucking cartoon character in love. Before that book, he was firmly on my side, ready to curse Eddie's name until the end of time. Now, he's one-hundred percent Team Eddie. *Fuck my life.*

"Pass the sugar, asshole," I tell him without bothering to address the elephant in the room. He does with a dramatic sigh, slamming the glass sugar container on the counter next to me with a loud clunk.

"I don't know how you can still be mad. The man wrote you a two-hundred-paged apology. I can't even get a guy to return a text."

"I'm not mad."

And the truth is, I'm not. Sure, Eddie was a lying jackass, but nothing he did was willfully malicious. I know he never meant to hurt me, he's just an idiot. And while I'd rather trim my nose hair with a weedwhacker than admit it to Jesús, I still love him. No matter how hard I try not to, how much I try to forget, it doesn't go away. Every night I go to bed thinking it will be different and each morning I wake up feeling like something is missing. *I am a fucking marshmallow.*

"Then why won't you go to him? Fall into his arms and make beautiful, snarky little babies!" Jesús vibrates with excitement, desperate for a happy ever after, even if it's not his own.

"Because it's over. We're done. Let it go, Casanova." I absentmindedly dump half a cup of sugar in my coffee, stir it with more force than I need too and try to ignore the devil in me that desperately wants to grab Eddie by the collar and kiss him until it's all okay again. But I can't see how to get there from here. I don't know how to make that leap.

"He's not done, chica." Jesús flips to the end of the book, to the part I know by memory because it's carved into my heart. "'I wish I could tell you, reader, that this story has a happy ending. But that isn't up to me. It's up to her. Every day I'll sit and wait and hope she can forgive me. Because without my flame, I'm drifting in the dark.'"

I shut my eyes tight and focus all my energy on keeping my lip from quivering. *You will not cry in the middle of this shop.*

"Jesús, that is enough," Pops calls from the back table. He gives me a sympathetic smile and waves me over to sit with him. "How are you doing, kiddo?"

I shrug and stare into my coffee. "It'll get easier right?" I ask, eager for some reassurance. "Time heals a broken heart and all that bullshit?"

"Oh, sweetheart. Nothing heals a broken heart. Time just lets you get used to the pain until one day it feels normal to ache."

"Great." I wipe away a stray tear and stare up at the ceiling, annoyed and embarrassed.

"You still love him, don't you?" Pops asks, already knowing the answer. I nod, not willing to admit it out loud. "Then why are you torturing yourself? The both of you from the sound of that book."

"I can't. Too much has happened." I try to convince myself more than Pops.

"Darling, you don't burn your house down to avoid fixing a broken window." He reaches across the table and places his thin, wrinkled fingers on my forearm with a gentle squeeze. "And you don't give up on love because it gets a little hard. Kick and scream if you need to. But just don't give up."

"What would I even say to him?"

"The truth. I think he deserves that much."

"The truth? I'm not even sure what that is." I drop my head in my hands and wallow in my anxious uncertainty.

"Once you're standing in front of him, I have a feeling it will come to you."

Chapter Thirty-Five

Eddie

"Smile. You look like you're at a funeral instead of a book signing!" Benji says, giving me a good shake with his hands on my shoulders.

"Funerals are more relaxing. At least you know the ending." I never do public appearances. I hate being in front of people. I hate being the center of attention. A book reading and signing is pretty much my nightmare. The only thing distracting me from how much I don't want to be here is the idiotic hope that Jackie will show up.

I have been living in a perpetual state of agitated desperation since I dropped off a copy of my book to her last week. I don't know if she read it. Or if she got the flyer for this reading. For all I know, she ceremoniously burned it in the bathtub of her apartment to excise me from her life completely. Or fed it to the coffee grinder. Or created some weird literary voodoo doll with it to curse me with bad grammar for the rest of my life.

I want to believe she read it. I have to hope it makes a difference. That she sees I'd do anything to make this right. Even stand up in front of a room full of strangers and basically read my journal to them, the intimate details of how I fell in love with a fierce and feisty woman who changed my world.

"It's time, buddy." Benji has to practically drag me up on stage. It's not a stage so much as a podium in front of a few rows of chairs. I forbid Darla from publicizing this reading other than handing out some low-grade flyers around the neighborhood, so the crowd is mercifully small.

I search the small space for Jackie, my heart racing at the thought of seeing her again. But she's not here. Panic and despair overwhelm me. *She didn't come.* I turn to walk off stage. There is no point in subjecting myself to any of this if she's not here.

As if he's read my thoughts — or maybe just my body language — Benji is blocking my exit, glaring at me. I know he and Darla moved heaven and earth to get this book published so fast. I owe it to them at least to follow through. I steel my nerves, clear my throat and begin reading the few prepared sections I chose from my book.

'"The sick truth of falling in love is when you find someone absolutely amazing, you can't believe you're worthy of being with them. Love preys on your insecurities until you hate yourself for not being what they deserve. And you talk yourself into walking away from what you love. Who you love."'

"That's bullshit!" a familiar voice shouts from the crowd.

My face splits open with the widest smile of my entire life. I could cry from joy when I look up and spot Jackie standing in the back, a well-worn copy of *Hurts A Lot Like Love* clutched in her raised fist.

The horrified bookshop owner steps in front of me and tuts, "This is a reading, not a discussion group. Please be respectful of the author."

Jackie snort-laughs, and I fall even deeper in love with the cheeky woman.

"No, it's okay. I'm interested in her point of view," I tell the owner with a gentle smile before turning my attention back to Jackie. "Which part exactly? That I found someone amazing? Or that our insecurities drove us apart?"

"Clearly I'm amazing."

"Clearly," I agree with a sappy smile.

"The part where you claim I ran away like some weak little scaredy cat." She glares at me, and I just smile in return.

"How would you describe it?" I ask, genuinely intrigued and eager for her response.

"I made the smart move and walked away."

"You mean the safe move."

She ignores my barb and continues with her literary review. "And, while we're on the subject of things you got wrong, the part where you're the wounded lover, and I'm the unforgiving evil tyrant is complete horseshit too."

I step out from around the podium and lock eyes with her. The crowd and the rest of the world fade away. There is only Jackie, the all-consuming siren who commands my undivided attention. It takes every ounce of willpower I have not to charge toward her, wrap her in my arms and never let go. My heart is stampeding despite my brain telling me not to send out the wedding invitations just yet. *She showed up, but that could just as easily be to kill you as to kiss you.* But now doesn't seem like the time for caution.

"I feel like the book makes it pretty clear, I was the one who fucked up."

She shrugs. "I could use more groveling."

"I see. That can be arranged. Is there any part of the book you think isn't some form of animal feces?"

Jackie struts up the aisle to me, crisscrossing her long legs with each step as if walking a tightrope and torturing me with the curve of her hips. She's sexy and she knows it. The tightness in my slacks makes me painfully aware of all the parts of her I've been missing.

"I thought the dedication was cool, if a bit sappy."

She's only three feet away now, just out of arm's reach.

"It's the truth. You're the love of my life."

She cracks a small, tenuous smile. "Even if I torture you for the rest of it for being a lying idiot?"

Unable to resist any longer, I take two quick steps forward and wrap an arm around her waist so she can't escape.

"I'm yours to torture, Ignis," I whisper as I nuzzle against her. She doesn't pull away. Instead, she lets out a soft moan that undoes me. I claim her lips with all the pent-up passion that's been churning in my stomach since she walked away.

The small room erupts with applause and a few hoots and hollers.

"Five...ten... Thirty-minute break everyone. Then we'll start the book signings," Benji announces to the crowd as I drag Jackie back to the corner of the store.

"I love you," I sputter, breaking the kiss when we're finally alone.

"I know. You wrote a book about it," she teases. She grabs my shirt and pulls me down for another breathtaking kiss.

"I'm so sorry," I say, pulling away again and staring down at those beautiful eyes.

"I know, again, I read the fucking book."

"Jackie, I—"

"Would you shut the fuck up and kiss me already? I'm trying to give you your happy ending here!" she shouts at me, and I can't help but laugh.

I oblige and kiss her until we're both panting and clawing at each other. She has wrapped both her legs around my waist, and I have her pinned against the classics section. *Sorry, Tolstoy.*

"So when you say happy ending...?" I rock my hips into her, asking how far she wants this to go. I'm so in love with this woman, I'd take her in the middle of Times Square if she'd let me.

"No, although I like where your head is at." She reaches between us and palms my hard-on with a brilliant smile. "Pun intended. That's not exactly what I meant."

I tilt my head and cock an eyebrow. Her smile fades. She licks her lips and swallows hard like she's psyching herself up for something. She stares at my chest and holds her breath.

"I was thinking we could give this a real try." She slides her hands from my pants to my shoulders, squeezing hard.

"This?" I ask, mainly to make sure she's saying what I think she's saying and not just what I *hope* she's saying.

"Us. I want to make this work." Her gaze slowly glides up my face until our eyes meet. "I love you."

My heart explodes. I lift her up and twirl us around, shouting "Jackie Ryan still loves me."

She gasps and clings to me, but I won't let her fall.

"You're such a dork!" she simpers in my ear.

I set her down, but don't let her go. I've got a giant goofy smile on my face. I lean down and kiss her softly.

"And you love me."

"Urgh, you're never going to let me live this down, are you?"

"Nope. Not for the rest of our very long, very happy lives together."

Epilogue

Jackie
Four months later

The delicious smell of dark roast and the low hum of customers brings a smile to my face. Stepping into Beans & Dreams after nearly two months of not being here, I can honestly say I missed the place. *Just a tiny bit.* I have zero regrets about quitting and I think Pops was overjoyed when I gave him my notice, but between moving in with Eddie and all the hours spent getting my graphic design business going, I haven't even had the time to stop in and say hello. I talk to Pops every day on the phone, and Jesús sends me updates of his growing flirtation with Benji, but there is something different about not being here all day, every day. Much as it felt like a prison sentence at times, this place will always feel like home. Somehow both comforting and oppressive.

"There's our guest of honor," Pops shouts across the shop. "Fashionably late. As usual."

"Anticipation heightens the pleasure," Eddie calls back from behind me, his voice full of teasing mischief. He slides his hand into mine and gives it a knowing squeeze.

"Touché," Pops answers with a smile.

"What has happened to my sweet, innocent Khakis?" I turn to Eddie and simper.

"He's been corrupted by a deliciously naughty woman." He leans down and kisses me. It's soft and reverent, in juxtaposition to his sumptuous words. Unsatisfied, I grab a fist full of shirt and launch myself at him. My NSFW kiss involves tongue and groping. It's hard and hot and completely inappropriate. And perfect.

When I pull back, Eddie's hair is sticking up in all directions thanks to my roving hands and he has dark lipstick smeared across his wide grin.

"See?" he whispers. "My virtue never stood a chance against Ignis."

"And you love it," I quip before walking away. The sound of his deep laugh at my back still makes my heart go all warm and squishy.

I meet Pops halfway through the shop and wrap him in a big hug.

"We've missed you around here."

"Of course you have."

"Well, to be honest, Jesús and I have missed you. The customers actually seem rather pleased. Even relieved."

I poke him in the ribs. "Bite me. I'm fucking charming."

He laughs, more *at* me than with me, I think.

"And that's why we're all here to celebrate you."

At Glory's End, E.B. Jericho's — or rather Eddie's — last book in the *Sins of Tomorrow* series, is releasing today. My cover design has been plastered on billboards and in shop windows for weeks now. I'm still not used to seeing it out in the wild. I still can't believe I won.

No one knows Eddie is E.B. Jericho. Well, no one except our small group of trusted friends. So today is about me more than him, which seems a bit odd. But Eddie doesn't seem to mind. In fact, I think he prefers it this way. He'd much rather be the man behind the woman, which somehow makes me love him even more.

"Shall we?" Pops offers me his arm in a gallant gesture to escort me over to our little party to begin the celebrations. Instead, I balk.

"I'm going to grab a quick cappuccino first. I'll be right there."

"Audrey can bring it to you." Pops moves to flag down the new girl, or should I say woman. She's in her early forties, newly divorced and desperate to find herself. Pops has an affinity for the lost and confused. I smile at the sweet, but mostly clueless woman and feel a pang of kinship with her. And not just because we both make horrible coffee.

"Nah. No thanks. I kind of want to make it myself," I tell Pops, letting my nostalgia show through.

He kisses me on the cheek, gives me a knowing smile and returns to our group. I slip behind the counter and get to work. The movements are second nature to me, the pressing of the grounds, the steaming of the milk. There's a certain satisfaction in the monotonous routine. I can understand why I let myself get too comfortable with it.

I peek over the coffee machine and take in our eclectic little group in the corner of the shop. My mom is here in her standard pencil skirt and blazer, million-dollar smile in place. She's chatting with Benji, who looks fabulous whether he's in a bespoke suit or a sequin ball gown. Today, he's casual in jeans and a button-down.

Eddie's grandma is also here, and a bit surprisingly, so is his mom. Unsurprisingly, she checks her watch twice in the two minutes I'm watching her. My shabby-chic coffee shop isn't exactly her idea of a good time. Pops and Eddie's grandma are as thick as thieves, and I make a mental note to ensure they aren't getting up to anything too nefarious. With their powers combined, I shudder to think of the havoc they could cause.

Elizabeth and Austin even flew in for a few days to celebrate. Although by the hungry looks Austin keeps giving her, I have a feeling he'd rather be testing out the durability of the bed springs back at their hotel room. Seeing as how they are newly engaged, I can't say I blame him. Better get all the sex he can now — everyone knows marriage is the end of the line for the orgasm train.

Despite being a horndog, Austin is indulging Jesús' million and one questions about being a football player. Which, let's be honest, is just an excuse to spend time ogling Austin. There's a reason I nicknamed him Man Meat. I wouldn't have thought Benji to be the jealous type, but the way he's staring daggers at Austin proves otherwise.

It's an odd bunch, a smattering of old and young, professional and casual, friendly and annoyed. But for some reason they are all here. For me. And that feels pretty damn good.

"Excuse me." A shrill voice drags my eyes over to the front counter. It's the same self-centered businesswoman from months ago. Ms. Non-fat. I chuckle at the memory that seems like a million years ago. "I would like to order."

It isn't what she says, so much as the way she says it. That sense of wanton entitlement oozing out of every word. Before it would've been like jackhammers to my ears. Now? Now I just think it's funny.

I turn to face her, smile and take a long sip of my coffee. After a contented hum, I tell her, "Sorry. I don't work here."

"Coming," Audrey chirps while scurrying behind the counter.

I meet her eyes, wink and tell her, "Good luck. Feel free to use the *special* sauce."

Audrey chuckles and shakes her head.

Eddie lifts the counter divide for me and asks, "That feel good?"

"Yes. God, it's exhausting being so awesome all the time." I take another long sip of my cappuccino.

"I know, right?"

"Should we go join our group of lovable misfits? I can't believe you wrangled them all here just because I designed the cover of some silly book."

He side-eyes me, the corner of his mouth lifting in that playful smile of his. "Winning that competition was an amazing—and much deserved—accomplishment. Even if it is some garbage book written by a half-wit," he says with derision.

I'm all about sarcasm, but the self-deprecating humor doesn't quite sit right. Eddie is the most amazing author. I fell in love with his words long before I ever fell in love with him. I turn him to face me and let a rare sincerity slip into my features.

"You know it's amazing, right?"

He looks away, shrugs and blushes.

"Seriously, Eddie. Look at me." He slides his gaze to mine and the genuine pride filling them makes my heart melt. "Your books are amazing. *You* are amazing. We should be celebrating you too."

"We are. Kind of. Everyone is here to celebrate our six-month anniversary too."

"Six-month anniversary? Of what? We've only been dating like four and living together for barely two."

"You don't remember? I'm heartbroken." He clutches his chest in mock pain. The act dies quickly and instead he steps into me. He tucks a strand of my hair behind my ear and cups my cheek. His focus is intense and inescapable. "It was six months ago today that I walked into this coffee shop for the first time and found the love of my life in a snarky, sarcastic —"

"Oh, shit. You're not proposing, are you?" I mutter without thinking. I love this man. I mean, L-O-V-E *love* this man. But I sure as fuck am not ready for any I dos.

He stiffens, his entire body tensing while his face goes completely blank. *Fuck. Fuck. Fuck!* I just ruined it. Again! I'm mid-freakout, debating if I'd rather be engaged to Eddie or lose him — which isn't much of a choice, I'd put a ring on it in a heartbeat — when he cracks up laughing.

"Not with that attitude, I'm not," he manages to sputter out between fits of hysterical laughter.

"You're an asshole." I slap him on the shoulder when he doubles over in amusement.

"Sorry, I couldn't help it. No, this is not a marriage proposal, which I've now decided will be a very private affair."

"Thank fuck." I breathe out a sigh of relief, but also, if I'm honest, a tiny bit of disappointment. I'd never tell him, but I know I'm going to marry Eddie one day, just not quite yet. "I barely feel like I'm getting my shit together. I do not need one more thing I can fuck up at the moment."

"Don't worry. You're safe from any impending nuptials." He interlaces our fingers and brings my left hand up to his oh-so-soft lips. Keeping his eyes locked on mine, he kisses my ring finger and adds, "For now."

To my complete bewilderment, Eddie talking about proposing does unbelievable things to my lady bits. I clear my throat and try to empty my filthy mind so I don't ravage Eddie like he's the last male and I'm trying to save an endangered species.

"And just so you know, celebrating a six-month anniversary is like having a graduation from second grade. You can do it, but it's idiotic," I tell him.

"I think that might be your epitaph."

"Fuck off."

"Also a valid option."

"Why do I even bother with you, Khakis?"

"Because you're madly in love with me. Duh." He wraps both arms around my waist and pulls me against him.

"Good thing too, because otherwise you'd be *so* annoying. You're so not my type. The love and the sex. Those are the only reasons I keep you around."

"Awww, you're already writing your wedding vows." He leans down and kisses me on the tip of my nose. It's nauseatingly sweet, and I love it.

"If we're writing our own vows, yours better be so sappy and adorable they bring tears to my eyes. And I mean the good kind of tears." I poke him in the chest.

"I've been looking for a new writing challenge. But if I'm pouring my heart and soul out in front of everyone we know, I want you to paint a mural for our altar. Something that I'll remember forever."

"I could do that." The request puts a smile on my face.

"All right then. It's a deal." He plants a soft kiss on my forehead.

"Deal," I answer.

He pulls back and looks at me. "Wait, did we just get engaged?"

"Absolutely not."

He quirks and eyebrow in challenge.

"We merely agreed to the stipulations of a future wedding."

"Which is different how exactly?"

I tilt my head and think about it. "No jewelry is involved?"

He laughs and shakes his head before telling me, "Don't ever change, Ignis. You're exactly my type."

Want to see more like this?
Here's a taster for you to enjoy!

Single in Seattle: Reeling in Love
Gloria Herrmann

Excerpt

"I think we got it," Molly said confidently to the almost naked man standing in the corner, wearing nothing but a stark white towel draped across his tan waist.

"You sure?"

Molly nodded as she scrutinized her work. "Yeah, the lighting was brilliant. I don't think we could have done any better."

"If you say so. You're the expert with that thing." The model pointed at the large camera Molly cradled in her hands, the screen displaying the digital shots from the day of working with him.

Molly loved her job as a professional photographer. Her friends were insanely jealous. What woman wouldn't be? She spent her days in her studio behind the lens of her trusty camera, capturing sexy images of some of the most gorgeous men from all over the world. Either she was paid to travel to them or they flew to Seattle to have her work her magic. Authors in the romance industry adored her photos. Her attention to detail had won her awards over the years, but what she loved the most was bringing the characters from books alive. Sure, it didn't hurt to look at well-defined muscles and sculpted abs that begged to be touched and to know what was hidden beneath the scrap of cloth that usually covered these men, but that wasn't how the business worked. Her friends would argue it was just because Molly didn't throw herself at these scantily clad men that she was missing out on these valuable opportunities.

If they only knew how nervous most of these men were, their fragile egos stripped down for her. It took Molly the first half of the shoot to calm them, easing them out of their shells, getting them just to loosen up enough for the right shot. It was more like babysitting rather than staring at a buffet, despite what her best friends thought. Not all the models lacked self-confidence, however. There were some who would stroll in, look directly into the camera and own it. But, for the most part, a lot of the guys were unsure and needed coaxing. Molly often felt more like a counselor than the world-famous photographer that she was.

Today, the Seattle sun was shielded behind soft, white clouds, filtering its rays into her studio that overlooked the Puget Sound. Her tall, glass windows provided the most stunning views of the shimmering water and the bustling city. Molly had worked hard for this view. It hadn't come easy or cheap — or without her busting her ass to make her name known in the photography industry. She had the scars — mostly emotional, but scars, nonetheless — to prove the struggles she'd endured, climbing to the top. Now she was one of the most sought-after photographers. Models from all over the globe wanted her to shoot them. *New York Times* and *USA Today* bestselling authors and publishers almost begged for her to shoot their covers. They wanted the best and...well, Molly was. Her skills proved that she had something special and everyone knew it.

Not bothering to sit down at her desk — bending over, instead — to focus on the images she was uploading to her laptop to edit, she almost forgot to say goodbye to the model she had just worked with. It wasn't until he was standing close to her, now fully dressed, that she realized he was still in her studio. Having him near her like that shifted the atmosphere in the room. His dominating presence was invading her space, creating nervous waves in her stomach. She inhaled his expensive aftershave, looked up from her screen and smiled.

Molly managed to say, "Great shoot today. Thanks again."

Remember to breathe, Molly.

"Yeah, it was amazing. You're amazing." The man paused, running his fingers along his day-old beard, the perfect blend of refined and unkempt sexy. His voice was silky and oozed well-practiced enticement. Molly watched him stand still, contemplating his next move. She was tempted to grab her camera and snap another shot. The light was hitting him just right and his pose was thoughtful and natural. This man was gorgeous.

He turned his mesmerizing gaze toward her and asked, "Do you want to grab a drink?"

Molly swallowed. It wasn't the first time she had been asked out by a model after a shoot. Sometimes it was the result of having bonded over their frail vulnerabilities. Sometimes they figured she was as good a lay as any while they were in town — another stamp in their romantic passport, so to speak. Molly wasn't so sure about this one. He wasn't overly emotional or guarded about his body, nor did he seem to really desire her. *So, what is he after?* She watched him scan the large studio. There was her answer. This type of square footage didn't come cheap and he knew that.

"You know, maybe another time. I'm really excited to get this edited." Molly pointed at her sleek silver laptop, delivering a fake smile in hopes it would put him off.

He nodded and thanked her again as he saw himself out. *The nerve.* Molly rolled her eyes and released the air she had been holding in her lungs. While she was in mid sigh, her cell phone chirped.

"Hello," she answered, a little more gruffly than she'd intended.

"Wow, so what's with the 'tude, lady? Bad day?"

It was one of her best friends, Tiffany.

"Just got done working with a model."

"Well, then why do you sound all cranky? Was he awful? So good-looking that you couldn't handle it?" Tiffany teased, causing Molly to laugh and her mood to lighten.

"You know the type. He wanted to go out for drinks—"

Tiffany cut her off quickly. "And you said, yes, right? Because if you didn't, you honestly need to have your head examined."

"I'd have to say he was more interested in my real estate than me." Molly frowned.

"Like real estate, as in the prime location between your legs? You know, it's all about location, location, location, baby."

"I wish." Molly huffed in frustration. "No, more like the prime location of my studio."

"That sucks."

"Tell me about it. He was gorgeous and he smelled divine. He was totally your type — tall, dark and devilishly handsome."

She heard Tiffany's disappointment through the phone. "Really? Oh, I just don't know how you do it, Molly. I have to give it to you. I would simply come undone working with those gorgeous men and not taking advantage of them every chance I got."

Tiffany always acted like she was some aggressive sex kitten, but they knew the truth. She was actually quite timid, which was a huge reason why she was single. All three of them were single and not dating anyone special. It didn't usually work that they were unattached all at the same time, but they were now. Their other best friend, Mackenzie, was the mother hen of the group. Well, more like the bossy one — completely overbearing, but with an absolute heart of gold. She, too, teased Molly about her line of work, but Mackenzie loved being a teacher, as it helped fill her maternal void. They had biological clocks that had gone haywire over the last couple of years, but everyone had warned them as they entered the dirty thirties that baby fever would hit soon after, and it had for Tiffany and Mackenzie. Every time they passed a stroller, neither could resist the temptation of peering in to catch a glimpse of some infant swaddled in fuzzy pink or blue blankets. Molly? She had her moments. They were brief and passed quickly when she heard the wail of a newborn or the shrill sound of a tantrum from a toddler. That didn't tempt her to want to rent out her womb for nine months.

She looked at her spotless, chic studio. Her smile went deep into her soul, masking the want for a baby. Her space sparkled and gleamed with the afternoon

Seattle sunlight, illuminating sleek lines and utterly contemporary taste.

If she were being completely honest with herself, yes, she did indeed want a child, eventually. But Molly also realized she was missing a very important part of the equation—a man. She didn't want just a sperm donor, though she and her friends had discussed that over far too much wine and Chinese food one night, considering it as a last resort. That had left them laughing for hours. No, Molly wanted the real deal. They all did. They wanted a man—a sexy, successful and simply wonderful man. *Is that really asking for too much?*

Being single, especially in Seattle, came with its challenges. Molly thought the enormous Emerald City should be plentiful with eligible bachelors, but Molly assumed that, as with any place, being single was a mixture of bad luck and an overly detailed list of the personality traits she wanted in a boyfriend. As time passed, her list had grown a lot shorter. She'd crossed off quite a few of her must-haves and was looking to review her available options. Now she figured it was mainly the bad luck that was keeping her single. Molly had been unattached the longest out of her friends, who were more like her sisters. Tiffany had been on a dating spree recently, but Mackenzie and Molly had known that none of the guys were Mr. Right for their friend. Mackenzie also had a pretty extensive list of requirements for her ideal mate, and she was even more stubborn than Molly when it came to sacrificing the qualities she was willing to live with, so she dated very little.

"Well, since you didn't want drinks with that sexy model, how about meeting up with us?" Tiffany asked.

Molly smiled. Yes, a drink with her best pals she could do. "That sounds lovely, actually." She could use some cheering up. The best cure for her bruised ego was some quality time with her besties.

"Great. I'll pick up Mac and we'll swing by the studio and grab ya. Sound good?"

"Perfect. I have some edits I want to go through, so just buzz when you guys get here."

Molly said goodbye and hung up. She stared at the monitor in front of her, the images of the model in various poses looking back her.

* * * *

Lost in her work tweaking the images with an array of filters, Molly was so engrossed that she almost didn't hear the loud buzzing that echoed off the large studio walls. She got up quickly from her desk and jogged to the massive double doors to let her friends in.

"Jeesh, what were you doing? I have been ringing that dang buzzer for, like, *forever*," Tiffany complained as she slipped past Molly into the studio. Mackenzie frowned and hugged Molly.

"We've only been standing outside the door for a minute," Mackenzie assured her.

Tiffany walked over to one of the large windows facing the Puget Sound. The sun was setting, casting a tangerine hue over the haze of the city. "God, do you ever get tired of this magnificent view?"

Molly shook her head as she joined her, staring out at the glittery lights in the surrounding buildings that seemed to stretch up toward the sky. "Nope."

"Yeah, I didn't think so." Tiffany laughed as she faced Molly. Her dark hair was loose on her thin shoulders. Tiffany's large eyes were a soulful brown and she had the best cheekbones. Tiffany was gorgeous in a unique and completely unexpected way. Molly's brain acted as a camera, capturing shots of her friend's delicate features as the sunset cast a shadowy light on her face. Tiffany sensed what Molly was doing and threw her a pouty look.

Mackenzie stood next them. The willowy blonde towered over Molly, making her feel short and stubby. Mackenzie had the figure of a teenager, slim and athletic. Her sun-kissed hair was cut in a sleek bob, framing the sharp angles of her face. She was another beautiful woman. Molly couldn't help but snap mental pictures of Mackenzie, too. She searched Molly curiously with soft mocha eyes. They all had brown eyes in varied shades of the common color, but resembling their different tastes in coffee. Tiffany had the espresso, dark and bold. Mackenzie was more of an iced mocha with an extra shot. Molly's resembled the instant crap coffee variety that no one really liked. Molly hated her eyes. They were plain. Her friends had tried to convince her otherwise, but they both had spectacular depth and richness in theirs. Molly thought hers looked like a muddy puddle after a typical downpour in Seattle — watery, with a sad, muted tone. Nothing special.

"What's going on with you?" Mackenzie reached for Molly, concern swimming in her eyes and worry creasing her otherwise wrinkle-free face, the result of fabulous genetics.

Molly sighed. *Is there anything going on with me?* They usually accused her of being moody, but she was an artist. *Isn't that sort of the job description? Acting the part of the tortured soul?* They sure never let her play that role for very long.

Tiffany stared at her hard and added, "Yeah, you seemed cranky on the phone. So what's up?"

"I don't know. I mean..." Molly really couldn't explain how she felt. She had a blessed life. Granted, she had worked for it, but, regardless, she knew she was lucky. Happy? Well, that was a different ball of wax.

"Drinks. That's what we need." Tiffany perked up, her hand on her hip, taking a sassy stance. She reached for the oversized purse that was slung over her shoulder. A Louis Vuitton knock-off, but it looked as real as they came. It was their little secret. Tiffany dug around and retrieved a bottle of Prosecco, holding it up for them to all gaze at her prize.

"You were carrying that in there? Oh dear. Seriously, Tiffany," Mackenzie scolded.

Tiffany winked and answered with a wicked grin.

"I, for one, am thrilled our friend is lugging around a bottle. You never know when you may need it." Molly grinned happily at Tiffany. "It does make you look a little like a wino, but you're my favorite drunk."

"No, you have me mistaken. I'm fun, not a drunk." Tiffany defended as she moved toward a long table that was against the wall opposite the windows. "Besides, at least I bring the good stuff."

"I have an idea. Let's stay in. Want to order some food?" Mackenzie suggested.

"Yes, let's do that. Molly's got one of the best views in all of Seattle. Let's just hang out here," Tiffany replied while she peeled the label away to get to the cork.

"Chinese?" Mackenzie whipped out her cell phone and started to dial their favorite takeout.

"Hell, yes," Molly and Tiffany answered in unison.

These were her girls. It didn't matter if they stayed in or went out on the town. As long as they were together, they were guaranteed to have fun.

Shortly, they were seated around a large glass table that Molly normally used to lay out prints from shoots. They dined on their fill of chow mein, pork fried rice and more Kung Pao shrimp than any woman should ever eat. White cartons, soy sauce packets and chopsticks were littered around them as they chatted about everything — mostly about the lack of sex or romance in their lives. Biting into a crispy fortune cookie — her favorite — Molly surveyed her beautiful friends. She couldn't understand why any of them were single. Tiffany was gorgeous, sweet and sassy... What was there not to love about her? Mackenzie was stunning, witty and full of love... She had so much to offer. Then there was her. She knew she might not be the sexiest thing on the planet, but she was successful, caring and everyone constantly complimented her on how pleasant she was, even telling her she was sort of hot, especially when she wore her glasses. *So how is it that I haven't landed the perfect guy yet?* Cracking open another cookie, she read the thin slip of white paper. Bold red font stared back at her, reading, *'There is nothing truer than the company of friends.'* How right is that fortune?

More wine flowed and, to keep the mood light, Molly blasted the radio. She and her two best friends danced barefoot in the empty studio, singing their hearts out and putting on a drunken performance that could rival the best pop star's. Tiffany swayed her hips to the song. Mackenzie took a while to loosen up, but then started to bop to the beat. Molly busted out some goofy moves that reminded her of middle school dances, her favorite being the 'running man'. They laughed hard, clutching their sides when Tiffany took a spill on the slippery wood floor. In their feeble attempt at helping her up, they all ended up on the floor somehow, spread-eagled, staring up at the vaulted ceilings. Music continued to play, filling the wide and open space, but the mood had shifted. That was when the laughter died and the deep realness of their friendship was exposed.

"I love you, guys," Tiffany whispered, her dark tresses fanned out against the honey-colored bamboo floor.

"Me too," Mackenzie added softly.

Molly tried to swallow the lump that was forming in her throat, feeling tears starting to surface. "I love you both. Thank you for tonight."

They all stayed on the floor, listening to several more songs before Tiffany said, "God, this floor is killing my back. I feel old."

Mackenzie and Molly both laughed.

"And for the record, we *are* old," Mackenzie replied.

"I wanted to say the same thing, but figured I would tough it out until one of you cracked." Molly started to get up.

Mackenzie and Tiffany groaned as they eased themselves off the floor. Working quietly as a team, they cleaned up the remnants of their dinner.

"I would totally live here, Molly," Mackenzie commented as she tossed several cartons into a waste basket.

Tiffany was wiping up some sticky Kung Pao sauce. "Seriously. This studio is so fabulous. You need to let me move in here."

"I do love this place." Molly looked around at her kingdom. An enormous clear-glass shelf that held her many awards was against one of the walls. Expensive frames that contained some of her best work were hung precisely in the perfect locations. Various shades, light fixtures and tons of other photography gear were set up in one corner. The room celebrated her. It showcased all of her efforts but, more importantly, it proudly displayed her passion for this form of art.

After every last morsel was cleaned and the work space was back to being immaculate, they made their way back to the window. The sun had long since disappeared, leaving the city lights to twinkle silently as the three of them stared out at the busy traffic below.

"Thank you again, guys. I really needed this tonight."

Mackenzie and Tiffany linked their arms through hers as she stood in the middle.

She would be lost without them. They knew all her secrets and her fears. They had supported her during her moments of crippling self-doubt. They'd loved her when she was at her worst. They'd dried her tears when critics had given her harsh reviews. They were her cheerleaders. They'd pushed her to continue to pursue her dream so many times when she'd just wanted to give up. They had been the first to celebrate when she finally did become successful and had told her countless times how much she deserved it.

These women were more than just friends. They were her tribe, her sisters. They were Molly's everything.

Home of Erotic Romance

Sign up for our newsletter and find out about all our romance book releases, eBook sales and promotions, sneak peeks and FREE romance books!

About the Author

Amelia Kingston is many things, California girl, writer, traveler, wife and dog mom. She survives on chocolate, coffee, wine and sarcasm. Not necessarily in that order.

Amelia loves to write about strong, stubborn, flawed women and the men who can't help but love them. Her irreverent books aim to be silly and fun with the occasional storm cloud to remind us to appreciate those sunny days. As a hopeless romantic, her favorite stories are the ones that remind us all that while love is rarely perfect, it's always worth chasing.

Amelia loves to hear from readers. You can find her contact information, website details and author profile page at https://www.totallybound.com